WALL BOUND

Lost Island
——— PRESS ———

This book is an English edition of *Muurvast* by Ruby Coene, the Dutch
original edition, published in the Netherlands. Copyright © 2024 Dutch
Venture Publishing. This edition was prepared by Mel Torrefranca in
consultation with Jen Minkman.

Wallbound
Copyright © 2025 Lost Island Press

Library of Congress Control Number: 2025919416

ISBN 978-1-962876-10-0 (paperback)
ISBN 978-1-962876-11-7 (ebook)

This book is a work of fiction. Names, characters, places, and incidents
either are the product of the author's imagination or are used fictitiously.
Any resemblance to actual events, businesses, companies, locales or
persons, living or dead, is entirely coincidental.

Cover design by Stefanie Saw (Seventhstar Art)

Lost Island Press LLC
Oro Valley, AZ
lostislandpress.com

WALL BOUND

RUBY COENE

ONE

This is it. The end of my life as I've known it so far.

The number 144,000 flashes on my wristband and illuminates the bare, steel walls of the switch cell. When the number's glow fades, everything turns black again.

In.

Out.

My breathing rumbles through my ears, and the silence envelops me like a thick blanket.

Just seconds ago, four armed members of the Guard filled my cell, their feet shuffling, pens scratching notes. Hands plucked at me while tight faces watched. Without a word, they examined and disinfected every inch of my body, shaved my head, and tied a thin leather strap around my wrist. I changed into a standard pale-gray jogging suit. They took everything I had, then vanished behind the thick wall that slid shut behind me.

I'm sure all four of them are still standing there now, their weapons at the ready, eager to punish a reckless escape attempt.

I have nowhere to go.

In.

Out.

The switch cell is barely five feet by five. I stretch my arms out, and my fingers graze the walls of my temporary prison. I know it's a false sense of protection, but I let myself believe that at this moment, I am alone—and alone, I am safe.

In.

Out.

In.

Out.

I look up, and thanks to the blinking light of my wristband, I see a ventilation grid in the ceiling about seven feet above. It's the only thing that interrupts the cell's otherwise smooth, gray surfaces. I focus on the walls and consider whether I could scale them, but I know that even if I could, the grate is too narrow for me to squeeze through.

I adjust my breathing to the rhythm of my wristband's flashing, trying to regain control of my emotions like my dad taught me. I count the seconds—three beats to breathe in, five to breathe out—but it doesn't calm me down.

I'll only be in this switch cell for five minutes—I know that. But for some reason, it feels like an eternity. Five minutes is enough time for the Guard to set my wristband, lock me up, and wheel my cell into the Hangar. Five minutes is also enough time for every horrific story about what awaits me to claw through my mind. I have seen battered youths leave this prison in just their underwear—and those were the ones who made it out alive.

I need to calm down. I can't let them see my fear when the door opens.

144,000 minutes.

2,400 hours.

100 days.

The standard punishment for a minor offense.

With a trembling thud, the cell begins to roll down the tracks that lead into the Hangar. The crunching sound of iron on iron sends goosebumps up my arms. These are the final steps of my penance, right before my real punishment begins.

Just as abruptly as the cell started moving, it comes to a halt. Another sound replaces the grinding—a louder one that grates my chest, not my ears. Stone scrapes over stone as the Hangar's concrete wall opens to receive my cell.

I've seen enough educational videos about the Hangar to know what's happening just by listening. At least once a year in high school, we'd see footage of a cell creeping down the tracks of the switch corridor, thick cables pulling it toward the Hangar.

Once again, my cell moves with a jolt. I can barely hold myself up straight. Adrenaline courses through my veins.

Behind me, the scraping of stone against stone resounds again, and I know my five minutes are almost up. I bite my lip hard enough that a scab pops open. The wound bleeds, but the pain is all that keeps me from throwing my body against the steel walls, sobbing and screaming for forgiveness, begging them to let me out of here.

The Hangar's wall slides back into place with a dull *thud*. Despite my efforts to calm down, my heart beats in my throat. My only way out is hermetically sealed.

My wristband stops flashing, the numbers coming to a stop. I hold my breath as a vibration pulses through my arm. From now on, my numbers will count down, and with each drop, I'll be one minute closer to freedom.

I hear a loud *click* and, agonizingly slowly, the door opens for me. My heart beats louder, stronger, and I feel like I can't breathe. I must remain calm. I must not show weakness. I force myself to suppress my fear—as much as possible, at least. I focus instead on the emotions I know much better.

Anger.

Rage.

Aggression.

A sudden beam of light widens, shining into the switch cell. I blink and hold my hands up, shielding myself from the blinding brightness.

"*Five.*"

My panting breath hisses through my ears.

"*Four.*"

A computer voice slowly counts down the seconds I have left.

"*Three.*"

Quickly, I step out of the cell.

"*Two.*"

The cold from the floor seeps through my socks and into my feet.

"*One.*"

TWO
144,000

The light is blinding, and before my eyes can adjust, someone strikes me in the gut. I step aside and raise my hands to fight, but it's no use—the girl laughs and grabs my wrist, twisting it until I'm forced onto the concrete floor.

A searing pain fills my arm as the attacker reads the numbers on my wristband. "It's a Guppy. No use for her."

She has dark circles under her eyes and fiery hair that grazes her shoulders. I assume she's a year or two my senior—seventeen or eighteen, among the oldest here. She studies my face, her gaze lingering on my bleeding lower lip and the adhesive patch on my eyebrow.

For a moment, I see something in her tired eyes. Curiosity, perhaps? But before I can place the emotion, it's gone, and her contempt is back.

The redhead releases my wrist, and I shuffle back up to find four other girls watching us. My eyes dart between them, hoping to find a glimpse of empathy, but they cross their arms. Their message is clear: I'm not one of them.

"What's your name, Guppy?" another girl asks. By the way she speaks, I get a feeling she's the boss—there's always a boss. She looks the part too —tall, lean, with toned arms and shoulders. But what stands out most is her black hair. It's long enough to be styled in thin braids that cling to her scalp.

I gulp and rub my crew cut. She must have been here for a long time.

"Sin." My voice cracks.

"What kind of name is that?" The redhead looks me up and down.

I shrug. In situations like this, it's best to remain silent—I learned that a long time ago.

"Strip."

I stare at her, mouth agape, unsure if I heard correctly.

"Are you deaf? Get undressed, or I'll do it for you."

I look around for help, but the five girls surround me. I have nowhere to go.

My heart pounds between my ribs, and my hands shake as I tug the sweater over my head, inch by inch. My thoughts race in every direction. I can't win, but I also can't let this happen—whatever *this* is.

"Gimme," orders the redhead—but she yanks my sweater away before I can even obey her. "And now your pants."

A pale-faced girl chuckles. Her chestnut-brown hair is hardly longer than mine, and a soft pink warms her cheeks.

Shame floods me as I slide the pants down my hips. I have won fights before, outnumbered like this, but something tells me these girls are even crueler than my classmates.

As soon as I pull my feet out of the pant legs, the redhead snatches the fabric. In return, she forces a pile of gray clothes into my hands.

Another identical jogging suit.

I don't get it.

"Guppies sleep in the back." The tall girl with braids points to a corner across the Hangar.

I stare at her, clutching the suspicious jogging suit, dressed in nothing but my bra and underwear.

"What are you waiting for?" she asks. "Your mommy to come save you?"

I'd love to punch her in the face and tell her to stop talking about my mom *or else*. But the way the other girls line up around her tells me enough. I don't want to be on their boss's bad side—not if I want to survive in here.

I nod and walk between her and the redhead. It feels dangerous to turn my back on them, but I clutch the jogging suit tightly and force myself to keep walking like I'm not afraid.

They don't come after me, and as I near the other end of the Hangar, I finally let my guard down and take in my surroundings.

The Hangar is about the size of my school gym, but that's where the comparison ends. There are no climbing frames on the walls, no enthusiastic shouts. Instead of a sleek and shiny floor, this one is made of concrete with little divots here and there. I can't find any windows either. The only light comes from the cool lamps dangling from the ceiling high above.

I note two doors—the one the switch cell just came through, and another one on a different wall. I wonder if that could be my way out.

In the corner, I approach a group of grubby mattresses lined up in two rows of three. A handful of girls, with hair hardly longer than mine, sit slouched over on the beds. I force myself to breathe evenly as I walk toward the one free mattress left.

A girl around my age, sixteen, glances up at me. She has tan skin and brown hair that seems curly, though it's too short to tell for sure. A shadow of a smile hovers on her lips before she jerks the free mattress away, stacks it atop her own, and lies down on both.

I toss my jogging suit aside, a familiar scarlet haze clouding my vision. Even digging my nails into my palms can't suppress my anger. Not when I'm standing here in just my bra and underwear. Not after what they said about Mom.

Smugly, she stares back at me, and I yank the mattress out from under hers.

"What the—"

With a thud, she topples off onto the concrete.

A stabbing pain shoots through my forearm where the wristband digs in, but I'm too furious to care. All the anger I've been holding in for the past few hours flares up.

"Keep your paws off *my* stuff." I slam my mattress down and stand on it demonstratively.

From the floor, she looks up at me with raised eyebrows. A moment passes before the corners of her mouth curve upward, her roaring laughter echoing through the Hangar. From the other mattresses, girls glance our way with looks of annoyance and amusement.

"A *spunky* Guppy. Never too many of those." She rises and offers a hand. "Q, like the letter."

Hesitantly, I lean over and shake her hand. "Sin."

"Welcome. You're lucky." She nods at the mattress I'm standing on. "Nora had to sleep on the floor for a month."

A younger girl—who I assume is Nora—covers her face with her hands. She looks about fourteen, just a tad too old for the Children's Facility. I wonder what she did to end up here.

"Put this on." Q pulls out another jogging suit from under her pillow. "It's not very dry—things never get dry in here—but it's cleaner than what you got from Milou." She eyes the jogging suit on the floor, which the redhead gave me earlier.

I nod, slide the clammy clothes on, and sit facing her on my own mattress.

Q grins. "I'll introduce everyone, since they seem to have forgotten their manners." She gestures to two girls sitting next to each other with their backs to us. "Mia and Lynn, besties for life in prison."

One of them has dark skin and black, fuzzy hair covering her scalp. The other's white-blond hair has grown out just enough to soften.

"Mia's the one who rolls her eyes at everything and makes sarcastic comments."

"Seriously, Q?" The dark-skinned girl, Mia, turns and gives us an irritated look. "Let the newbie recover for two seconds before you inundate her with useless information, okay?"

Q laughs. "Told you, didn't I? And that's Nora. You'll get to know her later." She points to the younger girl, confirming my assumption. "And now—the grand tour!" Q points to the other corner on our side of the Hangar. "The shower room and toilets are over there. We don't have much toilet paper because the girls use it for all sorts of things. If I were you, I'd keep some to yourself after the weekly delivery. For the times you really need it, if you know what I'm saying." She grimaces.

"Back there is the kitchen, but don't get your hopes up. All the food has to keep for a week, so most of it is tasteless or downright nasty." Q points to the sliding steel door. "And then there's the yard, which wasn't added too long before I got there. Apparently, a total lack of sunlight and outdoor air isn't good for our health."

Interested, I sit up a bit straighter.

"Again, don't get your hopes up." She raises her brows. "That door doesn't open every day, and when it does, it's only for an hour at most. If you're not back in the Hangar on time, you'll get stuck outside. *Really* stuck, with no water under the blazing sun for God-knows-how-long. So don't try to pull anything crazy. And now for the sleeping quarters..."

Q is already moving on—I figure it isn't the right time to ask more questions about the door.

"The Guppies with short-term punishment are over here. The Long-Termers with long sentences are over there." Q points to the front of the Hangar by the switch cell door. Right next to where I entered are a couple of beds, half hidden behind a wooden wall. I count the five girls from earlier.

Good. If it boils down to a confrontation, our numbers are even.

"The Long-Termers have the best spot. Farthest away from the toilets and closest to the switch cell." Q pats her mattress. "I heard it took the first Long-Termers weeks to take all the beds apart and build that wall. But you know, time is the one thing we have more than enough of here. That goes especially for the Long-Termers." With a sigh, she lets herself fall back onto her bed.

My attention is still focused on that sliding door. The yard is my best shot out—if the Guard added it recently, perhaps no one has tried to escape through it yet. I *have* to try. Cross needs me out within a month.

Q gives me a solemn look. "I know what you're thinking about, and trust me, you're better off forgetting it."

How does she know?

"Just keep a low profile, okay? Especially for the first few days. I saw the way Rhea looked at you. You know, the tall girl with the braids? She doesn't take kindly to Guppies. Especially not Guppies on *this* side of the Hangar. If you're smart, you'll stay away from her."

I nod. I wasn't planning to cause trouble with Rhea anyway. I know better than that. While there are no official figures, rumor has it that only one in five young teenagers sent to the Hangar ever see the light of day again.

Ever since the Reflection Zone for Rebellious Youth—known as REZO—was implemented, people have called it inhumane, but only in whispers. President Vallance has squandered free speech, along with everything else that doesn't fit the image of a perfect Netherlands.

"This place isn't much, but we have to make do with it. At least for the next..." Q looks at her wristband. "58,340 minutes."

I do the mental math. Since Q is a Short-Termer, she was also given 144,000 minutes, meaning she's been here for almost sixty days—over half her sentence.

I study her with renewed interest. She looks so calm, like her only responsibility is to serve her time.

That's a luxury I can't afford. I have to get back soon, for Cross.

He needs me to stay alive.

THREE
143,056

I wake to the sound of a girl breathing through her stuffy nose. The hairs on the back of my neck stand up, and I can't keep my heart from racing. Even with my eyes still closed, I know I'm not alone—her rattling breaths are far too close for comfort.

I force myself not to flinch when my wristband sends a tingle down my arm. She hasn't done anything to me yet, so I assume she's waiting for me to wake up. I have to keep pretending that I'm asleep.

Carefully, I peek through my eyelashes. It's still dusky in the Hangar, but through the haze, I see not one, but three pairs of legs at my bedside.

The stuffy girl chuckles. "Look! Guppy's pretending to sleep." She must have heard my breaths quicken.

Lying down puts me at a sharp disadvantage. I need to stand.

In a single, fluid motion, I jump out of bed, planting my bare feet apart in a solid stance.

Relief washes over me—the girl who spoke isn't Rhea, though I recognize her pale face from the other side of the Hangar. She was the one who chuckled when the redhead—Milou—ordered me to strip. Her sweater is bunched up on one side, revealing a bit of her tummy, and her chestnut-brown hair is slightly grown out.

My breath hitches when I notice the janky piece of wood in her hand— it looks like it came from a broken bed.

My eyes dart to the two girls behind her. They, too, are holding pieces of rough wood.

While I know I can't win this fight, I force myself to grin at the pale-faced girl.

"What are you smiling at?" She takes a step toward me, one hand propped on her waist and the other clutching the wood. Not the smartest move—her whole midriff is exposed. But I don't do anything. *Yet.*

"Are you slow? I asked you a question."

From the mattress nearby, Q sits up. She looks at me, then at the pale-faced girl, before rolling her eyes. "Seriously, Lindsay? This again? Haven't you learned by now that bullying isn't gonna win Rhea's respect?" She scrambles to her feet and stands beside me as backup.

Her support feeds me confidence. I clear my throat and mutter, "No."

Lindsay gives me a puzzled look. "No *what*?"

"No, I'm not slow. You asked if I was, right?" I know it's stupid, but I can't help myself. "Or did you forget already? Are *you* slow?"

Lindsay balls her fists. "If I were you..." She trails off when I step forward, every cell in my body poised for a fight.

"If you were me, *what*?"

I ignore the shock in my forearm. The real danger stands in front of me.

She bares her teeth. "If you wanna get through your 144,000 minutes alive, you better follow our rules."

"How can I follow rules I don't know? And who are *you* to tell me what to do?"

"The rules are simple." Rhea pipes up, emerging from the darkness with Milou at her side. "So long as you keep a low profile, you're following them just fine."

I turn so I can monitor both groups at once.

Rhea gives me a grim look, her voice laced with threat. "If you want to get out of here, learn to adapt."

A shiver rolls down my spine, but I stare back at her anyway.

For a few seconds, the Hangar falls silent. Everyone seems to be holding their breath, waiting to see which of us will break.

But then I remember Cross.

I gulp, forcing my eyes to the floor. I have to hold back. For him.

"That's what I thought." Rhea's words crack through the air like a whip. "This Gup isn't gonna cause any trouble."

She turns to go, but Milou lingers with her arms crossed, waiting for Lindsay's group to follow.

As Lindsay leaves my bedside, her tense shoulders tell me that our feud isn't settled. It's only a matter of time before she'll try to assert her dominance again, and maybe next time, she'll wait until I'm alone.

Once Milou disappears with Lindsay's group behind their makeshift wooden wall, I sigh and sit down. Rhea might be the star of the show, but Lindsay's the one gunning for me.

"What's her problem?" I ask.

Before Q can answer, every light turns on, and a shrill, beeping noise echoes through the Hangar.

I frown and look around. *Now what?*

Q answers my unspoken question. "New supplies."

With a scraping noise, the switch cell door slides open. The Long-Termers don't spare a moment before attacking the new stuff in the cell. Milou stands facing us, hands clenched at her sides, her hair as fiery as ever, challenging us to object to their power. As if she *wants* us to give her a reason to fight.

"Once a week, the Guard delivers new supplies," Q explains. "Toilet paper, detergent, dish soap, bottles of water and food. And the phones, of course. Occasionally they add some extras, like new towels, underwear, bras, sanitary napkins, or approved books. One time they even threw in strawberry tarts—in honor of President Vallance's birthday." Q almost licks her lips at the thought. "Of course, the Long-Termers devoured those before we could get anywhere near them, but I got to lick three of the wrappers." She sighs deeply. "I miss whipped cream."

"Phones?" I'm still stuck on that part.

"Yeah, they don't tell you that in the promo videos, do they? There's no universal basic income here. We have to work for our food."

Rhea shouts, drowning out Q's words. "Supplies for the kitchen!"

The Long-Termers carry armfuls of items to the kitchen and showering rooms.

"Toilet paper!" Rhea calls out next.

I watch as two-thirds of the toilet rolls disappear behind the Long-Termer's wooden wall.

Within a few minutes, they've finished their plundering, and all that's left in the switch cell is one lone box.

Mia, the Short-Termer with dark skin and ringlets, runs after it with an identical box in her arms. She trades one for the other.

"Those are the phones," Q explains. "It's our job to disassemble them and sort out the reusable parts. Then, at the end of the week, we return them all sorted—otherwise, the Guard cuts our supplies."

Mia joins us with the new box and sets it on the floor.

Q removes the lid, revealing a whole pile of smartphones. "It's boring work, and the tools we get are made of plastic that break every five minutes, but a girl's gotta do what a girl's gotta do."

"Yeah, they're obviously not gonna give us real tools." Mia grins. "Otherwise, someone would end up sticking a screwdriver in Lindsay's neck."

FOUR
143,022

"Shh." Q scowls at Mia, then nods toward the shower room, which Lindsay and one of her buddies are just leaving.

"Have fun working!" Lindsay calls out, strutting our way. "Let us know when you're done. Maybe we'll let you into the kitchen by then." Her friend laughs, and the two of them sashay away, hips swiveling.

"What's her problem?" I ask again.

Mia chuckles. "I don't think my remaining 80,000 minutes would be enough time to list off all her problems."

"Lindsay's the most recent addition to the Long-Termers," Q explains. "I think she's trying to prove herself to them or something. And we're allowed in the kitchen whenever we want, you know. The Long-Termers have already taken away all the good stuff."

"I'm really not afraid of Lindsay," I say. "She just gets on my nerves."

Q shakes her head. "Lindsay's not the one you should be worried about. Believe me, you don't want to make enemies here. Rhea's right—there may be five of us, but we're still at a disadvantage. You've seen their weapons. You draw too much attention to yourself by acting all confident." She sighs. "And attention is *not* a good thing if you want to get out in one piece."

Her warning makes me think of Cross—his bright, blue eyes and his wild, blond hair. He's my entire world, and he's in danger. I have to get out of here.

I clench my teeth as another stab jolts through my wrist.

Q grabs a phone and a tiny plastic screwdriver. "You have to learn to hide your emotions."

"Huh?"

She nods at my wristband.

Apparently, I'm not hiding the pain as well as I thought.

"It's the Guard's way of keeping us under control without having to invest in cameras or guards. Every time your heart rate goes up, the wristband gives you an electric shock. A small increase only results in a tiny jolt, but if you get really worked up, it could actually knock you unconscious. It's the ideal way to stop fights before they get out of hand, but by now, most of the girls have found a way to deal with it."

I stare at my wristband, my mouth agape. "They never told me that."

Q snorts. "Of course not. People know better than to talk about it on the outside. No one wants to take that risk."

I shudder. Some places are much worse than the Hangar.

"Not even Vallance would get away with torturing children," Q continues. "And admitting that his *great plan* didn't work out so great isn't gonna happen either."

I look at Q in horror. There is so much we don't know.

"You'll be fine. So long as you don't forget what's waiting for you outside, you'll find a way to survive in here."

As if I could ever forget about Cross. He's the reason I'm here.

Although it was just yesterday, it feels like an eternity since I last felt the sun on my cheeks.

"Keep reading." I set my eight-year-old brother up on the couch with a stack of old comic books. "I'll be back in forty-five minutes, tops."

I planted a kiss on his head, locked the front door behind me, and stepped into the gentle sun. It was a beautiful day—hotter than it usually is in March, but it tends to get hotter earlier every year.

I welcomed the change as I walked half a mile to the nearest dock for a shared bike, taking in the sights and sounds of spring—the bright green of newly budding leaves, the irregular brown bark of tree trunks, a flash of red and the soft whistle of a bird looking for a place to build its nest...

After reaching the dock, I cycled for about fifteen minutes toward my targeted hospital depot. They're usually poorly guarded since people aren't dumb enough to steal medicine. There's usually no need for that kind of theft. The Dutch government regulates healthcare efficiently—if you fill out a form online, you get a call from the doctor the next day.

But thanks to the one-child policy, my parents never registered my little brother.

It's not a life-or-death law or anything. The Guard doesn't round up second-born children and throw them into pits of fire. It's just an incentive that gives families with one child extra resources—a way to promote a smaller population, and therefore less pollution.

If you *do* have a second kid, you miss out on the extra child support, and you have to buy anything that isn't strictly necessary out of pocket. It doesn't sound like a big deal on paper, but Dad claims to have heard of families who registered extra children and ended up hassled by the Guard. According to him, that's the *real* penalty of not following the one-child policy—the reason my parents didn't register Cross.

It would have been fine to skirt the law for a healthy kid. But for one with diabetes, their choice turned the one-child policy into an *actual* life-or-death situation.

Since my brother doesn't legally exist, he can't access the healthcare system. My parents' initial solution was to bribe a physician to examine him and smuggle us a huge supply of insulin. But soon after, she vanished —and with her, so did our supply line. Rumors claim the Guard lifted the doctor from her bed in the middle of the night.

I'm glad Dad insisted on giving her a false name for Cross. Everyone knows the Guard has their ways of getting information out of people— even the ones you think you can trust.

The doctor's smuggled insulin, while helpful, wasn't everlasting. Once we ran out, I tried a number of times to raise my own sugar levels so I could get insulin for him legally, but that only resulted in sore, bleeding fingers and garbage pails full of puke.

And that led to my current solution—stealing from hospital depots. This new errand of mine was surprisingly easy, and it seemed to have become a permanent solution. I wasn't worried in the least as I biked toward the depot yesterday. I simply pedaled, relishing the sun on my cheeks and the wind in my ear.

Suddenly, the bike chain jammed, and I flew head-first into the soft shoulder of the road.

My knees stung, and a warm trickle of blood ran from my brow to my cheek. I groaned and pushed myself up, glancing over at my crashed bike. A thick branch stuck out from between its spokes, and a large dent flattened the front wheel.

I wiped the blood away and picked up the broken bike. I needed to reach the closest dock to exchange it for a working one. It would take forever to drag this piece of junk there, but I had no other choice.

Normally, I'm not careless; I moderate everything—cameras, guards, possible obstacles—but by the time I reached the hospital depot with a new bike, I was sweaty and eager to get home for a shower. I snuck inside without a second thought, my head low to avoid the cameras, and walked straight to the medication shelves.

I noticed the sound too late—quiet footsteps, right behind me. When I turned to dash off, two strong hands locked around my arms from behind.

My heart hammered in my throat as I yanked myself free and tried to shield my face in the process. If the cameras were to recognize me, it wouldn't matter if I escaped or not.

"Don't move!" The man's voice echoed through the depot.

My toes curved into the soles of my sneakers as I sprinted away. I heard his footfalls behind me and picked up my pace. A cramp burned my side, and my breath wheezed, but thankfully, he was losing ground.

The depot fences loomed in the distance. I was almost out.

Just a bit further...

My fingers curled around the fence, and I started to hoist myself up.

A taser jabbed the back of my neck, and suddenly, my muscles froze.

No!

My head struck the ground with a thud, my stomach lurching. A cry escaped my tight throat as the guard pulled my arms behind my back, locking my wrists together with cold metal handcuffs.

I failed. I didn't get the insulin for my brother.

And now, because of me, he might not survive.

FIVE
142,662

I'm back at home with Cross. He's reading a comic book; I'm reading a novel. It's warm—but just for a moment.

I'm pulled out of my dream by someone shaking my shoulders.

I groan and turn away.

"Sin, the showers are free. You coming?" Q holds out a towel. She stands at my bedside, along with Nora, and I know she won't take no for an answer.

From the moment I entered the Hangar yesterday, Q has made it her mission to befriend me. She follows me around like a chattering, faithful shadow, but I know friendship might not be her ultimate goal. People are stronger together than alone, and surely she knows that.

Regardless of her motive, I'm grateful for her company. I can't come up with an escape plan until the door to the yard opens, and her constant chit-chat makes the wait bearable.

With a sigh, I haul myself out of bed and take the towel.

In the shower room, I leave my clothes on a shelf in the main corridor and step into a cubicle. The door ends a couple feet above the tile—and if I stand on my tiptoes, I can peek over the top—but at least it offers a semblance of privacy. The shower room is actually one of the few images of the Hangar made public. It's a way for Vallance to look like he cares about our dignity.

A weak stream trickles from the shower head. I put my hand out to feel the water. Lukewarm. It's honestly better than yesterday, when the pressure was fine but the water was icy.

I stand as far back as possible to catch the water, twisting into an awkward pose so I don't brush the wall or step on the grimy drain. Next door, Q sings softly in her cubicle.

"I belong with you, you belong with me. You're my sweetheart."

I grin when I hear the lyrics of an old Lumineers song through the thin wall separating our cubicles.

"Love we need it now, let's hope for some. Cause ooooh, let Linds be nice."

She butchers the melody and swaps *we're bleeding out* for Lindsay's name, which makes me chuckle.

"Shut up, bitch!"

My eyes widen. I recognize that voice.

Q stops singing.

I press my ear to the cubicle door and listen. Whispers echo in the corridor on the other side. The tension I washed off comes back with a vengeance. Something's not right.

Taking half the time I normally need to rinse the soap off my body, I wrap a towel around myself and step outside.

Lindsay and two other Long-Termers are holding my clothes.

"Not so tough when you're naked, huh?" Lindsay jerks her head as she turns and leaves the shower room. The other two follow her out.

"Okay, that sucks." Q pops up beside me, her face covered in water droplets. She's wearing a soggy jogging suit. "You want to borrow Nora's spare?"

I hesitate. While it's tempting, I know that next time, Lindsay will think of another way to torment me. The girls at school were exactly the same. The only way to beat them is to prove that you're not afraid.

"No thanks. I'll get my own stuff." I'm about to strut off, but Q grabs my arm.

"Please don't, Sin. It's not worth it." She shakes her head, shooting a concerned glance at the open archway Lindsay's group just left through.

"I'll decide for myself what's worth it." The words come out snappier than I intended.

"You're not just jeopardizing yourself if you do this," Q hisses. "You can't win this fight."

Oh? We'll see about that.

I yank my arm free, and, with long strides, leave the shower room to approach Lindsay. She stands in the middle of the Hangar now, partly shielded by the two girls on either side of her. My clothes are in a pile on the concrete floor next to her bare feet, and her glare dares me to steal them back.

I take a deep breath and cross my arms without covering my hands, ready to defend myself if necessary. "I think you accidentally took *my* clothes."

"*I* think," Lindsay mimics my voice, "you were told not to cause trouble."

"Believe me, Lindsay, I'm definitely not looking for trouble. But you have something that belongs to me." I try to sound as calm as possible and keep my arms still, despite the stabbing pain from my wristband.

Lindsay crosses her arms, and I can tell from the glint in her eyes that my efforts have failed. "Come and get it."

This is the moment she's been waiting for—the moment to assert her dominance. If I walk away, I'll come across as weak, but if I jump her and she grabs the towel, I'll be exposed in my birthday suit. Both options give her what she wants. She wins.

But the joke's on her—I'd rather be naked than weak.

"Okay, then," I reply, and a hint of doubt flickers in her eyes.

Looking more confident than I'm feeling, I step forward and bend to grab my clothes, holding my towel with my other hand.

I keep my gaze on Lindsay. Her lips are pressed in a tight line, but she does nothing.

When I turn, I feel someone tug on my towel. The rough fabric slips from my hand, falling to the floor, and all I can do is press the clothes against my body to cover myself as much as possible. I look around as jolts of pain twitch through my wrist.

Lindsay holds up my towel and looks at me challengingly.

"Well done, Lindsay," another girl calls, laughing.

Grinning, Lindsay drops my towel. "Oops."

My gaze flicks to the fabric on the floor, but I decide to leave it there. With my head high, I turn my bare buttocks toward them and head for the Short-Termer section.

"Hey!" Rhea yells.

I pause and look over my shoulder to see a fretful look on Lindsay's face. But it's *me* that Rhea and Milou stare at scornfully. Gosh, why didn't I listen to Q? Dad warned me often enough that my stubbornness brings me more trouble than good.

"I thought we had an understanding." Rhea eyes my naked body with disdain. "I thought you weren't going to cause any trouble."

I bite my lip to hold back my rebuttal. That *I'm* not the one causing trouble—that I'm just trying to mind my own business while Lindsay makes that impossible.

In a few strides, Milou leaves Rhea's side and stops in front of me. She towers at least four inches taller, and without clothes, I feel incredibly vulnerable—but I still return her scowl.

Her hand shoots forward, grabbing my neck, her long fingers clawing around it.

I can't breathe. A rasping sound escapes my throat, and black spots dance before my eyes.

I try to push her away. My left arm shakes uncontrollably as the wristband sends stronger electric shocks through my body. My clothes fall from my shaky grip to the floor. My nails scrape her skin, but it's not enough to make her loosen her grip. My head goes fuzzy.

"Enough, Milou." Rhea sounds bored.

The redhead finally releases me. I fall to my knees, gasping, struggling to breathe while tears run down my cheeks. With each intake of air, my fear diminishes, replaced with humiliation.

"Consider this your last warning," Rhea says, and whips around to leave. Milou, Lindsay, and the others follow her to the Long-Termer section.

I force my breaths to steady as I return to my own group. I'm not out to pick fights with anyone, but I still feel satisfied when I hear the distant hissing of Rhea telling Lindsay off.

I flop onto my mattress and turn my back to Q.

"Oh, hell no!" Q grabs my shoulder and turns me to face her. "There's no way you're getting off that easy!"

SIX
142,648

"You really have no idea, do you?" Q's eyes spit fire. The other Guppies echo her rage, casting me angry looks from their mattresses.

"What are you talking about?"

Q's eyes narrow. "You're making it worse. You need to think before you act."

"Seriously?" I lean in, raising my voice. "*You're* the one who said it was good to have some Guppies with spunk. *You're* the one who was singing that stupid song about Lindsay."

"How was I supposed to know they'd walk in at that precise moment? If I had, I wouldn't have done it. But you deliberately went after her, looking for trouble." Q rolls her fingers into fists. "You really have *no* idea what effect your behavior has on us. You're not alone in here, Sin. The Hangar is made up of two parts. Them and us. There is no *me*. What you do affects us too. I thought you understood that."

"How could I?" Another shock fills my wrist. "I wasn't given a manual when I wound up here—when those bastards took me away from everyone important."

"We *all* have people on the outside, Sin." Q scoffs. "Don't you get that? If we want to get out of here alive, we have to lay low. We can't beat the Long-Termers. We only have our fists, but they have sticks, planks, and... *Milou*."

"So you just let yourselves be kicked around?" I meet eyes with the other girls.

"We choose to keep our distance as much as possible," Q answers. "When we don't bother them, they don't bother us."

"But Lindsay started it..." Even I can hear how childish I sound.

"But you could have ended it." Q shakes her head. "I get that it's hard, but you'll have to adapt if you want to survive here."

"Anything you can think of, we've already tried," Lynn adds. Of all the Guppies, she's been in the Hangar the longest—in a few days, her time will be up. Her white-blond hair sleekly frames her defiant, green eyes. She rattles off a list while ticking off her fingers: "Ambushing them in their sleep, blocking the shower room, challenging them to one-on-one fights. Everything always ends up causing more damage to us than to them."

Sitting beside Lynn, Mia picks at a scab on her arm. Q was right about them being friends—I've never actually seen them *not* in each other's company.

Mia looks up at me. "Did you know that Milou used to be on the national youth kickboxing team?"

"Even Milou is afraid of Rhea," Lynn adds.

"Well I'm not afraid of anyone," mutters Nora, the youngest Guppy. I find myself wondering, once again, what she did to end up here.

"Nora's a tough one, but even *she* agrees that it's not a good idea to antagonize Rhea or Milou. Right, Nora?" Q looks at her insistently.

Nora makes a bored face. "Whatever."

Q looks back at me. "So promise this won't happen again."

"Fine." I give in. "Here endeth the sermon?"

"If you think *that's* a sermon, you should meet my father." For a second, something dark flashes across Q's face, but then she exhales deeply, and smiles at me. "But now we're all in agreement, so yeah, sermon's over."

With a sigh, I roll onto my stomach and try to push my thoughts of everything in the Hangar out of my head. What replaces it is not much better. Things are turning out exactly the same here as they used to in school. Why doesn't anyone seem to understand that I'm not here to fight? Certainly not by myself against an entire group of girls. I'm not stupid.

I grimace as I think of the last time I faced a group of girls by myself. I lost big time, and that was *with* my clothes on. Some girls from class had waited for me after school, seeking revenge since the teacher chewed them out for bombing our group project. Naturally, they blamed me for it. As if it was *my* fault they couldn't carry their weight. I never wanted to work with them in the first place. I much preferred flying solo. Still do.

I vaguely remember the girls screaming and storming off when one of the teachers interrupted our fight. I got an earful for causing trouble yet again, even though I didn't start it.

More vividly, I remember the proud look on Dad's face when I came home covered in bruises.

"A father can't help but encourage his daughter when she knows how to fight like a rhino in distress," he'd proclaimed. I can't suppress my smile when I remember his many strange sayings.

However, his pride vanished two weeks later when we received a gray envelope in the mail. The letter from Social Services addressed my many quarrels and expressed concern about my upbringing. One more offense, and I'd be taken from home and placed in a Children's Facility. According to our president, the boarding schools in the Northern Netherlands were the ideal environment to *redevelop* children who lacked proper parental guidance.

Dad reported me sick for a week and taught me how to suppress my anger, how to ignore the dancing red spots in my eyes.

"You have to learn to be as calm as a koala, as quiet as a turtle, and as controlled as a beaver rat."

"Koalas are *not* calm. They're just stoned stupid from eating all that eucalyptus," I objected, but I knew my dad was right. I had to get my act together.

After that, I never fought again. Not until I ended up in the Hangar, at least.

I pull the pillow over my head. I don't want to hear anything or see anyone. I just want to get out of here.

FROM OUR ARCHIVES:
Senior citizens left to their own devices!

From your correspondent Roger Vallance

Disturbing numbers from anonymous sources were made public yesterday about expenditures at the nursing home Peaceful Gardens and the Midwest Judicial Complex.

Government spending per capita is roughly 10 times higher for prisoners than for elderly residents in nursing homes. Our parents and grandparents —the people who built the country we live in—are being sidelined by their own government.

While criminals enjoy private rooms and recreational activities, many elderly care facilities deny residents the basic human right of privacy. We've heard first-hand accounts of four or more people crammed into a single room, with nothing but a thin, portable screen set up between them as they're being washed.

We're just as shocked as you are. The Party for the People will not sit idly by while politicians mistreat our elders.

For more information on what you can do, click here!

378.4K likes
15,355 comments
1,678 shares

SEVEN
135,294

The number on my wristband seems frozen in time. Although my brain knows that it only takes a minute for the number to go down, it feels as though the countdown is growing slower and slower. And who's to say it isn't? For all we know, the Guard could've programmed them to cheat.

It's day six, and the door to the yard still hasn't opened. The longer I wait, the more empty I feel. Normally I'm busy taking care of Cross and Dad, keeping myself under control at school, and planning my next drug run. Now there is nothing to occupy me. I don't even feel any anger or fear like I did when I first arrived. Instead, I feel restless. There's this constant sense of urgency that I have to *do* something.

From my mattress, I listen to rain fall on the metal corrugated sheets that make up the Hangar's roof. The monotonous tapping of raindrops, which has been going on for hours, reinforces the lonely feeling of the outside world moving on without me.

My fingers sort through the reusable parts of the phone I just took apart: gold, copper, silver, aluminum. I never knew there were so many different metals in one simple smartphone.

Like the rain, the monotonous work doesn't calm my mind. Again and again, I have the same thoughts, the same questions.

How much insulin does Cross have left? Enough for a month—maybe a month and a half?

Did Dad make the wrong decision by choosing not to register him?

I realize now how much I lost when I entered the Hangar. All control, all choices, my freedom, my family—I lost everything. The Guard hopes that in 100 days, I'll realize how wrong I was to break the rules of our glorious country.

In an effort to distract myself from questions without answers, I practice Dad's breathing techniques. I make a game out of slowing my heart rate every time my thoughts raise it. The wristband's shocks—or lack thereof —are a good way to measure my progress.

Dad would have loved it if I practiced these breathing exercises so diligently back at home. But even when it comes to the fights I got into before the letter from Child Services landed in our mailbox, I have no regrets. I only fought when I had to stand up for myself. I won't give that up. The Guard can't take my sense of justice away from me.

With a sigh, I toss the screen of a phone into the bin.

Dad used to talk about life before President Vallance—how young people who didn't obey the law were subjected to community service so they could make up for their wrongdoings by helping the community they'd harmed. Such a rightful system sounds like a fantasy. With the Netherlands' ever-growing resource shortages, especially of rare earth metals, Vallance alone benefits from the phone-dissecting work we do here. Not the nation. Not the community. Just Vallance.

Who knows how much he makes by selling these parts on the side?

President Vallance changed everything once he came into power. He's even the reason I'm here. Thanks to Vallance, anyone between fourteen and eighteen who breaks the law is sent to the Reflection Zone for Rebellious Youth—either for a hundred days or a full year, depending on their crime. The schools I attended always played footage of REZO's opening every year on its anniversary. Vallance called it a testament to the Netherlands' greatness: *"We don't punish the youth; we give them a fresh start."*

REZO's industrial shell looked better suited for storing fighter jets than people, so soon enough, people started calling the bare-bones building the Hangar. There are ten of them now, scattered across the country—six for boys, four for girls.

According to the textbooks we read in school, REZO isolates young people from evil temptations, allowing them the opportunity to find their better selves. It's an empty, barren space to reflect on your sins—away from your friends, your family, and anyone else who might have a bad influence on you.

Once upon a time, I believed what they told me. It sounded like a good idea. No one in the Hangar was bumming around. But back then, I didn't know anything about the wristbands or the phones. I didn't know anything about what it's *really* like in here.

Dad always expressed doubts about the so-called *opportunity* the government made REZO out to be. If someone isn't old enough to drive a car or drink alcohol, how could you expect them to be mature enough to make choices that will affect the rest of their lives? How do you choose what's right when you don't fully know what *right* is?

Yet the completely revamped justice system seems to be working, if you look at the numbers. According to news reports, crime rates have plummeted over the past thirty years. But according to Dad, it's come at a cost. There is no more noise pollution, but there are also no more young people laughing in the park. No more trashed bus shelters, but also no more teenagers busking in the streets. Dad always talks about his childhood with a big smile on his face. I'd give anything to go back in time and walk down the streets with him during those days.

But the numbers don't lie, and most people only look at statistics.

With a sigh, I remove the last bolt from the phone I'm working on. My thoughts are driving me crazy.

The sound of scraping concrete resounds through the Hangar, and instantly, everyone sits up straight.

The door to the yard creaks open, slowly but surely. This is the moment I've been waiting for.

I force myself to stand casually. I don't want Q and the others to predict what I'm about to do.

Mia leads the way. "Finally. I was dying of boredom. You're all so *lame*."

"*I'm* not boring," Q replies, catching up to Mia. "You were the one being quiet these past few hours."

The bright sun blinds me when I step through the door.

The heat is overwhelming, and the dry ground bites my bare feet. Already sweating, I squint around. The yard is a lifeless sandbox surrounded by steel-plated masonry walls about ten feet high—tall enough to be unclimbable, but low enough to mock.

I wonder who came up with the brilliant idea of calling this a *yard*, because there isn't a single blade of grass in sight.

The other Guppies sit in the shade of one wall while I take in every inch of the yard. My stomach tightens as the realization sinks in—these walls are impossible to scale. The metal's probably scorching from the sun.

But when I curl my toes, a smile brushes my lips. The sand yields more easily than I expected.

Going up isn't an option, but going *down* might be.

Finally, I join the others and sit next to Q. Every Short-Termer is here except Nora, and I look around, observing the small group I've found myself in. Apart from our matching jogging suits and cropped hair, we're as different as can be—a haphazardly thrown-together mess driven here by circumstance. While they chat, I run my fingers through the sand, deeper and deeper. I expect to reach something hard, but I don't.

"Sin?" Q looks at me questioningly, and when I meet her gaze, she bursts into laughter. I realize far too late that they've been trying to talk to me. "Clearly, our great chocolate bar debate is too advanced for you."

"Sorry." I try to stick to the conversation, but when it drifts back to *milk or dark chocolate*, my mind wanders again. I've only had chocolate once in my life. We couldn't afford it, but one time, Dad gave me and Cross a piece of milk chocolate each—left over from a banquet at the zoo. It melted on my tongue, and I'm almost certain I groaned out loud when I tasted it.

The three girls look at me open-mouthed when I tell them the story.

"I can't compare," I say, "but the milk chocolate was *so* good, I can't believe there's anything that could top it. My vote goes to milk."

"But"—Q waves her hands around—"there's more cocoa in dark chocolate, and cocoa *is* chocolate, and more chocolate is always better."

"How do you come up with this nonsense?" Lynn rolls her eyes. "Popcorn contains less corn than regular corn, but it's the salt that makes it delicious."

"That makes no sense *at all*. Popcorn is just as much corn as regular corn." Mia raises her eyebrows. "And anyway, popcorn is supposed to be sweet."

Once again, a discussion erupts, and this time, I can relate. Popcorn is one of the few treats we ever had at home. Cross loves it. Sweet or salty, it makes no difference to him—as long as he can stand by the pan and listen to the kernels explode.

"Popcorn with chocolate really is the very best." Q licks her lips, staring dreamily ahead.

Lynn scoffs. "Just how rich *are* your parents?"

Q's face tightens. She presses her lips together and inhales a sharp breath.

Lynn doesn't notice her agitation and keeps prattling on, running a hand through her white-blond hair. "If *my* parents could afford popcorn with chocolate, I never would have ended up here."

"You don't know anything about me," Q snaps. Without a final glance, she gets up and storms back into the Hangar.

"Whoa. I didn't mean to..." Lynn's words linger between us like soap bubbles. She gives Mia a pleading look, hoping for backup.

Mia grimaces with a shrug.

The tension is palpable. I try to distract myself by digging further into the sand, feeling for a steel plate that maybe—just *maybe*—isn't there.

A wave of relief washes over our group when a shrill beep calls us back inside.

As we head in, I look over my shoulder at the little pit I dug by the wall. I finally have a goal—something I can *do*.

Mia raises a brow when she notices my hole, but she doesn't comment on it. She probably just assumes I was fidgeting in boredom.

Right when we enter the Hangar, I notice something off—the red light above the switch cell corridor starts flashing, and the other concrete wall slides open next.

EIGHT
135,346

Rhea, Lindsay, and the other Long-Termers run to their sleeping quarters before darting to the switch cell, brandishing wooden clubs. I try to keep my eyes on the corridor, but with them lined up side by side, I know I won't be able to see much.

Q gets up and stares at the five backs blocking our view. "Another Guppy." There's a tremor in her stiff voice, like she's trying—unsuccessfully—to sound stoic. "Normally, they never send people in such quick succession." She looks at me. "You haven't even been here for a week."

The red light stops flashing, and the tinny voice counts down from five to zero.

I can barely hear the Long-Termers as they greet the newcomer, but I keep a tense eye locked on their backs.

It feels like an eternity passes before Rhea steps aside. "Over there," she says, pointing at us.

Across the Hangar, a new Guppy starts toward us. She looks about sixteen—same age as Q and me—and she's dressed in only a bra and underwear. The Long-termers must have taken her fresh jumpsuit too. Her arrival mirrors mine, but the fear plastered on my face when I arrived isn't on hers.

Two bright blue eyes land on me, wearily but proudly, set in a narrow face full of freckles.

"I'm Frankie." The new girl joins us, her eyes darting to Q as she offers a hand.

"Q." She shakes Frankie's hand. "And that's Lynn, Mia, Sin..." She points to us one by one before gesturing to the mattress where Nora lounges. "And Nora—she's having a bit of an off day." Q looks back at Frankie. "I'd give you my spare jogging suit, but Sin's already wearing it."

"It's too hot to wear clothes anyway." Frankie shrugs, looking down at her bra and underwear. "I'll just wash these later."

"Whatever floats your boat." Q plops onto her mattress. "Sin also took the last mattress, so until Lynn leaves, you can sleep on the floor—or with me."

"Q snores like a baboon," Mia teases. "But you can hear her from across the Hangar, so I guess it doesn't matter anyway."

"The floor's fine." Frankie sits next to Q on her mattress. "I've slept on worse."

"Okay then. Over there, you'll find the shower room and the toilets..." Q rattles off the same introduction to the Hangar she gave me less than a week ago, but before she can finish, Frankie places a hand on Q's thigh and smiles. The gesture comes so naturally to her that it seems like the two of them have known each other for years.

"I know where everything is," Frankie interrupts.

I tilt my head, studying her. Every citizenship class in the Netherlands shows the same informational REZO videos once a year—we learned how each facility is constructed and the process before someone is sent in. The videos are always accompanied by an overenthusiastic voice discussing the importance of this new step for our justice system. But those videos alone don't show enough for someone to know where *everything* in the Hangar is.

Frankie shrugs, sensing our confusion. "My father has an important government position, and I have the password to his laptop." She smiles again. "I knew that sooner or later, I'd end up in the Hangar, and I wanted to be prepared. Plus, it's pretty easy to memorize the floor plans, since it's just a box, and every facility is built the same. One perfect design. Lather, rinse, repeat."

My jaw drops. I've never heard someone speak so lightly about the Hangar before.

"But..." I try to ask her what she means, though I only get one word out before she interrupts.

"My father and I disagree on just about everything. Me being here is his worst nightmare." Frankie's eyes turn glassy, and a long silence passes before she continues, her enthusiasm back. "What about you girls? How did you all end up here?"

No one says a word. Part of me wants to point out that Frankie hasn't even told us what *she* got arrested for, but another part wants to stick to the unspoken rule that we don't talk about our crimes.

Lynn and Mia stare at their bare feet, but Q doesn't take her eyes off Frankie.

"I was trespassing," she says, her stare cold.

That's exactly what my file says too, but I'm certain our stories are completely different.

"Same here," I admit. Q nods at me.

Frankie rolls her eyes. "All those stupid rules, right?"

Mia and Lynn gasp in unison. Q whips her head around to see if the Long-Termers overheard Frankie. *No one* says stuff like that out loud. Never. Not in public, at least, and being careful about what you say isn't a habit that vanishes when you end up in the Hangar.

Hearing criticism of the government was only something I ever heard in the privacy of my own home. Even before Cross was born, my parents questioned new policies, like how President Vallance was trading more and more elements of our old culture for things that suited him better. Our democratic system that was so solid on paper was becoming a mere shadow of what it once was. Remarks considered treason outside of our home bubble were traded at the kitchen table with ease. My dad knew he had nothing to fear when we were indoors. Even Cross didn't set foot outside until I was old enough to know when to keep my mouth shut. No matter how angry I was, my dad's words stayed a secret whenever I talked with my fists.

Absent-mindedly, I rub my knuckles, and when I look up, I stare straight into Frankie's eyes. Earlier, I thought they were bright blue, but now I notice darker rings around her irises, gray spots clouding her gaze. She has stormy eyes. Just like Cross's.

Q looks at her wristband as if it's a watch. "I'm gonna get food. Anyone hungry?"

"I'm starving!" Frankie laughs, running a hand over her freshly buzzed, blond hair. "Normally, the washing and shaving only takes a few minutes, but I guess I'm a special case. It took forever, and they didn't give me anything to eat."

I can't tell if she's joking or being serious. With me, everything happened so fast. A few hours after the taser hit me at the depot, I was already in the switch cell.

The three of us make our way to the kitchen, where Rhea and Milou are piling their dirty bowls in the sink. I keep my distance, sticking to the other side of the room as I grab a corn roll from one of three small, refrigerated pantries. I hold the bread between my hands to heat the rock-hard thing, then spread watery cherry jam over it with a plastic spoon.

"Hmm, that looks delicious." Frankie sniffs and snatches the sandwich from my hands. "How sweet of you to make this for me."

"Hah." I smirk. "As if."

Frankie winks. "I don't mind you being even sweeter." She slings an arm around my shoulder, her hip pressed against mine.

"No!" Rhea's voice cuts through the kitchen, like she's correcting a domestic dog.

In a flash, Milou shoots across the room and grabs Frankie's arm, pulling her away from me.

Frankie screams as Milou twists her arm behind her back and forces her over the countertop, pressing her head into the wood.

Rhea joins us, clutching a wooden pole. "Keep your paws to yourself."

"It was just a joke." Q raises her hands in surrender. "She didn't mean anything by it."

"No one *ever* means *anything*." Rhea's face tightens. "Those words let far too many people get away with stuff. But not here. Not when I'm in charge."

Milou kicks a low cabinet, and the door pops open.

My stomach contracts as I realize what she's about to do.

"I didn't mind it," I blurt out, my voice trembling. "Frankie didn't do anything wrong."

Milou grabs Frankie's wrist and lines her fingers up against the cabinet edge.

"Stop lying," Rhea says through gritted teeth.

I gasp as Milou kicks the cabinet door shut. It slams against Frankie's fingers, and a louder scream erupts from her mouth.

Milou releases her, and Frankie slumps down onto the tile, leaning back against the cabinets. Her eyes water as she cradles her swollen, red hand.

Rhea glares at Q. "Get your newbie under control. Next time it won't be her fingers."

NINE
135,266

I rush to help Frankie up, turn the faucet on, and hold her bruised hand under the cold water.

"Was that *really* necessary?" I ask, frowning at Rhea.

Q looks at her too, frustration brewing in her eyes.

"Yes. Necessary." Rhea leans on her wooden pole, her voice turning to ice. "I'm keeping us safe. If anyone can do whatever they want, this place will turn to chaos. No one here is innocent."

"Exactly!" I exclaim. "And neither are you!"

Rhea spits on the floor in front of me. "Don't talk about things you don't know."

"I know enough." I ball my fists, my self-control slipping away. As soon as I step forward, Q grabs my arm and tries to pull me toward her. But I'm stronger and manage to free myself.

I run after Rhea, black spots dancing before my eyes.

I don't even see her move before a sting lances through my shoulder.

I whimper and try to launch my own attack, but Rhea strikes me again first. My knee is on fire and I collapse to the kitchen floor. Pain shoots through my entire body, stemming from my knee and wrist. I know I don't stand a chance.

Q kneels beside me—probably to help, in part, but mostly to prevent me from being stupid and going after Rhea again.

"Anything else?" Rhea looks at me sternly.

I keep silent as Q holds me down.

"That's what I thought," she adds, turning to leave.

While Rhea and Milou head back to the other Long-Termers, Q helps Frankie and me to our sleeping area. Frankie isn't doing too bad, but the swelling and redness in my knee only worsens. Mia and Lynn plop down next to us, and Nora stands hesitantly.

"Is there anything I can do to help?"

Q smiles at her. "Could you wet some towels with cold water?"

Nora nods and runs to the shower room.

"It's not fair. Frankie didn't do anything wrong." My voice is just a whisper. "Rhea says she wants it to be safe here, but she's going too far."

I have no idea what went on here before I came, but from how everyone walks on eggshells around Rhea and obediently follows her rules, I know it couldn't have been good. I do it myself—conforming to what she wants. I let it happen.

Nora hands one soaked towel to Frankie and presses the other against my knee. We thank her, and she sinks onto the mattress beside Q with a sigh.

"We're never going to learn, are we?" Nora says, resting her head on Q's shoulder.

"No." Q closes her eyes.

"You *shouldn't* learn. It's not fair." Frankie rolls her non-injured hand into a fist. "Everyone wants to use power to make things better, but the moment they get a taste of that power, it becomes more important than anything good. It's no different in here than it is out there."

Mia and Lynn look at Frankie with disapproval.

"Vallance buried years and years of fighting for equality, all with his stupid lists." Frankie's words sound exactly like my dad's. He never agreed with registering people on government lists—databases that track everything from behavior to family background. Lists like that are almost always used against you, not *for* you. Everyone knows getting registered can ruin your life. That fear is what keeps people in line.

Frankie sighs. "I'm sure almost everyone here is on some kind of list."

She's right. I'm on the Social Services register thanks to all my fights.

"Maybe what you're saying is true," I say, "but sometimes self-preservation is more important than speaking out." *Sometimes I should heed my own words*, I add to myself.

Frankie looks at me. While she says nothing, her unspoken questions burn my skin. Does she blame me for what happened in the kitchen? For prioritizing myself, and only helping her *after* Milou finished her punishment? Does she think I'm a coward?

My jaw clamps as I remove the wet towel from my knee. Red bruises bloom on my pale skin.

Q looks at me with pity. "She got you pretty good."

I nod, and with a wince, place the towel back on my knee.

"Rhea knows how to take someone out." Q leans back onto the mattress. "I heard she and her boyfriend committed robberies. I think she's the one who terrorized Vallance Park."

Everyone's heard the stories about people getting attacked in Vallance Park. It was always a man and a woman, targeting couples on dates. The man would beat up the guy, and the woman would hold down the girl, forcing her to watch. Everything was taken from them: their money, their jewelry, their sense of security...

Of course, the news never mentioned those attacks. Stuff like that doesn't officially happen in our country. But rumors are too frequent and too similar to be a coincidence.

Mia sits up a little straighter. "I heard Rhea was caught because she wanted to protect her boyfriend. She literally threw herself at the Guard so he could escape. The only reason they didn't try her as an adult is because they hope she'll give him up once she does her time."

"Vallance has too much faith in REZO." Q slumps down and rests her head on Nora's leg. "As if any of us here really ponder our sins. If she didn't give him up back then, she sure as hell isn't gonna do it months down the line."

Lynn rolls her eyes. "It's all stupid gossip anyway."

Mia falls silent, but my thoughts pick up where her story ended. What if Mia and Q are right? Would they have tried her as an adult if nothing more was to be gained by keeping her here?

The finalized Work Provision for Criminals plan was proudly presented several years ago. The WPC looks like an oil rig in the middle of the ocean the Netherlands borders on. Today, the tens of thousands of solar panels, wind turbines, and hydraulic turbines on the platform generate much of our country's energy. It is an energy supply that is expanded, maintained, and improved upon by convicts under the guidance of a small group of trained professionals. I heard that working on the WPC for five years could earn you enough money to retire.

"Two birds with one stone," Vallance had proudly proclaimed. *"A cleaner and safer country for everyone."*

Once on the platform as an adult prisoner, you never get off. Children and teenagers get a second chance, but adults don't deserve one. People call the WPC the *Drain*, since they use it to flush away waste nobody wants.

Stories have come out from people living on the coast near the Drain who had to clean up swollen corpses from drowned prisoners washed up on their shores. Rumors say the bodies had protruding ribs and inexplicable scars.

A shiver runs down my spine. I shake my head and notice Frankie staring at me.

"Should I drench the towel in cold water again?" Nora asks.

"No thanks." I force a smile. "I'll hobble to the bathroom by myself. If I don't start moving my knee, it'll get worse. Plus, I want to show Rhea that she can't push me around so easily."

FROM OUR ARCHIVES:
Politicians ignore facts on our aging population

From your correspondent Roger Vallance

Politicians choose to ignore the ominous figures on our aging population and pay no heed to the impending disaster that will affect us all.

According to figures from the CBS, by 2040, more than a quarter of the population will be over 65, and of those, a third will be over 80. The enormous strain this will place on the already overburdened elderly care system is hard to estimate, but one thing is certain: something must change. More money must go into elderly care—a lot more. Our elderly deserve a dignified winter of their lives.

It is time for action!

Last Friday, over 5,000 of our supporters carried out symbolic thefts at shops within a one-mile radius of the Binnenhof, the heart of our government. With banners and signs, our message was impossible to miss:

> *Want to take a shower every day? In prison, you can!*
> *Steal something. You'll be better off.*
> *Life in prison beats assisted living*

In a silent march, we delivered the stolen goods to the Binnenhof—piling up chocolate bars, milk cartons, shoes, suitcases, bicycles, and even a mannequin in the courtyard until the police shut us down. Seventeen were arrested.

This is only the beginning. We will be heard.

For more information on what you can do, click here!

TEN
133,997

"Only twenty-two minutes to go." For the umpteenth time today, Lynn walks up to us, trailing a hand through her white-blond hair. "How far in advance should I get ready, you think?"

"It's about a seven-second walk from here to the switch cell," Mia mocks. "So I think you have at least twenty-one minutes left."

Lynn steps back, eyes wide.

Q slings an arm around Mia and pulls her in for a hug. "Lynn's gonna miss you too. And you still have Nora, Frankie, Sin, and me."

Mia growls. She refuses to meet Lynn's gaze.

Lynn bites her lip and walks away—to the toilets, to the tracks of the switch cell, to the kitchen, then back to us.

The sense of impending freedom has completely taken hold of her. Apart from her short nights of rest, she's constantly on the move, looking for something she can't find. It's as if she is stuck in a nightmare, a bad dream in which she wants to pack her suitcase, but all her things have been taken away.

Her restlessness keeps the rest of us occupied. Again and again, our conversations drift to the outside world.

"Know what I'm gonna do first when I get out of here?" Q looks at Frankie and me, but she doesn't wait for us to reply. "I'll take a cab to the nearest Beasties Burgers and order the greatest Beasties Barbecue Broccoli Burger, with extra ketchup!" She closes her eyes, folds her hands around an invisible burger, and pretends to take a bite.

Frankie laughs, rolling onto her side so she can see us better. "Did I ever tell you how I got banned from my local Beasties?"

"No." I shoot her a surprised look.

Q laughs. "And all this time, I thought you were *so* sweet! That you took a wrong turn and accidentally wandered into the Hangar."

"Hah! There's so much you girls don't know about me." Frankie winks.

"I believe that, yes, but tell us what happened," I urge her.

"Okay. So I was in Beasties with two friends of mine—let's call them Pim and Pom."

Q rolls her eyes. "You and your code names."

"I have to respect people's privacy, especially when I'm talking about things they could get in trouble for," Frankie says. "So anyway, Pom had already ordered at the counter when she realized she didn't have enough money to pay. Without saying anything, we ate our food. Then, when the waiter arrived with the check, Pim stood and puffed up his chest.

"'The check?' he asked. 'You're bringing *her* the check?' he pointed at Pom. 'Don't you know who she is? That's Porta Vallance. The one and only daughter of our honorable president.'"

"Porta?" Q cocks an eyebrow. "That's not the name of the president's daughter. It's—I don't know—something pretentious. Like Ivanka, or Bianka, or something."

"It's just another code name, okay?" Frankie sighs. "For some reason, the waiter didn't believe us. He called the Guard, and we had no choice but to run. It took two weeks for me to gather the courage to go back to that Beasties again, and once I did, I saw a *Wanted* sketch of us on the window. Fortunately, it was so poorly drawn that even my own mother wouldn't have recognized me. But I didn't go in, just in case."

She chuckles, but Q and I stare at her, jaws dropped.

"Why would Pim claim that Pom is Vallance's daughter?" I ask. "Of course the waiter wouldn't believe him!"

Frankie shrugs. "You never know. Vallance goes through lots of trouble to keep his daughter out of the press. Why not take advantage of the fact that no one knows what she looks like? Don't you agree, Mia?"

"Fuck you, Frankie." Mia leans back against the wall, a dark expression crossing her face. She's been in a pissy mood ever since the number on Lynn's wristband dropped below a hundred. I can't place whether her friend's imminent departure triggers jealousy or loneliness.

"Four minutes left." Lynn is back again.

Mia exhales a sharp breath through her nose.

"I'll miss you, Mia." Lynn smiles at her friend, who still won't look at her. "Maybe we can go for a drink together once you're outside too. It won't be much longer."

Doubt laces her words. We all know they won't meet up in the future, no matter how close they've become. Once people leave the Hangar, they want to forget about it as quickly as possible—and besides, the Guard is always watching. Two former teen inmates hanging out would draw too much attention.

I flinch when the tracks carrying the switch cell begin to hum.

Mia squares her shoulders, finally offering Lynn a hesitant glance. She opens her mouth to speak, but nothing comes out.

"Well, enjoy your freedom." Q grins but doesn't bother to stand. "Enjoy an extra juicy Beasties Burger on my behalf!"

I step toward Lynn, and she shakes my outstretched hand. Words aren't necessary.

Frankie hugs her next. "Good luck, and thanks for the mattress." She pulls away from Lynn, walks to my side, and rests her hand on my shoulder. Even through my thick sweater, I feel the warmth of her skin on mine. I'm surprised my wristband doesn't shock me.

Nora hugs Lynn and tucks something small into her hand—I can't see what it is.

"Mia?" Lynn steps toward her, but Mia turns her head away.

Her words are thick. "Just *go*."

"Okay," Lynn replies, her voice hardly more than a whisper. She turns and walks toward the switch cell door, where the Long-Termers line up in front of, arms crossed. They're blocking her way.

Horrified, I turn to Q. "What are they doing? They can't *stop* her, can they?"

Q grips my arm like a warning. "They're *not* stopping her, Sin. It's only a tradition. You don't want to get involved."

Frankie stiffens, her fingers clasping my shoulder even tighter.

Finally, Lynn stops in front of the line of Long-Termers. The concrete wall slides away with a grating noise as the switch cell enters the Hangar.

Once it's fully inside, the wall slides back into place behind it, and the switch cell door opens, inviting Lynn inside.

"Sixty."

"Fifty-nine."

The mechanical voice echoes through the Hangar.

"Fifty-five."

"Fifty-four."

Rhea and the other Long-Termers leap forward, and Lynn pales as the group circles her.

"Fifty-one."

"Fifty."

My stomach lurches when I hear a dull thump, followed by a yelp. The Long-Termers punch and kick Lynn wherever they can manage. They force her arms up, tear off her clothes. Crying and screaming, Lynn fights to get to the switch cell.

Q digs her nails into my skin to stop me from interfering, but her efforts aren't necessary. There's no way I'd ever get involved in *that*.

"Thirty-six."

"Thirty-five."

As soon as Lynn manages to break free from their clawing hands, everything shifts. The Long-Termers split up into two lines, forming an honorable pathway between them for Lynn to pass through. It's some kind of fucked-up final tribute.

With her head held high, Lynn limps through the final stretch before turning toward us. Her left eye is swollen and a trickle of blood runs from both her eyebrow and her lip. Her forearms are covered with scratches where dozens of nails have torn open her skin. Yet still, she manages a weak smile of farewell before stepping into the switch cell.

"Three."

"Two."

"No!" Mia's desperate cry echoes in the Hangar as she runs from us, racing after Lynn.

"One."

Frankie's fingers are like a vice around my shoulder.

"Stop!" Q screams and runs past me, but she's too far to catch Mia. Way too far.

A beep echoes through the switch cell just as Mia reaches it.

I try to tear myself from Frankie's grip, but she's too strong.

Time seems to slow as Mia leaps forward, reaching out for Lynn.

But just as she reaches the switch cell's door, a shriek fills the air. Mia's arm shoots up uncontrollably. Her entire body convulses, and a wet stain appears between her legs.

Lynn watches her best friend collapse just outside the cell.

I gasp when Mia's head strikes the concrete floor.

Crack.

Lynn stands petrified in the switch cell, her eyes quivering. "I'm sorry," she croaks, tears streaming down her cheeks.

With a bang, the cell door slams, stealing Lynn from our sight. The Hangar's concrete door opens to devour the switch cell next, leaving Mia on the floor, lying like a corpse.

ELEVEN
133,922

Q, Frankie, Nora, and I run to Mia as the Long-Termers quietly leave the scene.

Q reaches Mia first and kneels, dropping an ear to her lips. "She's still breathing. She'll have a killer headache when she wakes up, but she should be fine. Help me carry her to a mattress. It's all we can do for her."

The four of us lift Mia to our corner of the Hangar.

For a long time, we sit in silence, watching her lie unconscious. We've already taken apart and sorted this week's phones, and weirdly enough, I miss keeping my hands busy.

Finally, Frankie breaks the tension. "I'm gonna do laundry. You coming, Sin?" She holds her hand out, offering to help me up.

I take it. Doing anything is better than sitting here anxiously.

When we reach the toilets, Frankie starts collecting the dirty clothes we've piled up in the corner. "I knew it wasn't possible to escape through the switch cell," she says, "but I had no idea it worked like *that*. I expected the Guard to just... catch you outside and send you to the Drain."

"I still don't really know what happened." I sigh, filling a sink with water. "It was all so fast."

Frankie joins me and loads a pile of clothes into the sink, her eyes glistening. "The wristbands are an interesting piece of technology. They track your heart rate, transmit electric shocks, and have a GPS system embedded.

I always thought they were tuned to an area a few feet outside the edges of the Hangar." She presses her lips together and begins to scrub. "But apparently they're more accurate than that. Mia's wristband zapped her as soon as she reached the entryway to that cell. And hard, too. There must be a sensor in the doorway that our wristbands respond to."

Frankie wanders off into her own thoughts, so we do our laundry in silence.

Because our tracksuits are thick, cleaning them is tough—especially the wringing part. They dry slowly too, and always seem to stay a bit damp. Must be the air in here.

I wring the fabric until my arms hurt, welcoming the burning sensation in my hands. It makes my head pound a little less, if only for a short time.

The next morning, I wake to an alarm blaring through the Hangar. I roll onto my side and press the pillow against my ear, hoping to block it out.

But the shrill beeps are still ear-shattering.

The switch cell enters the Hangar again, and immediately, the Long-Termers rush over. Rhea distributes the new stock at lightning speed.

Finally, she holds up two hefty books, reading their titles aloud for us. "*History of Our Democracy. Handbook: Dealing with Guilt.* Nothing else." She throws the tomes aside and walks off.

Only the tray filled with new phones remains in the cell.

With a sigh, Q stands and walks over to exchange the old tray for the new one.

The cell door slides shut, locks itself, and rattles backward on the tracks.

Q brings the tray to our corner, puts it down, and sits next to Mia, who is deathly pale—but finally conscious again.

As I disassemble the first phone, Nora approaches the books. She looks around, picks up the thickest of the two, tucks it under her shirt, and returns to her mattress.

I watch Nora curiously as she sinks into a cross-legged position and carefully tears pages out of the book. Once she has an entire stack, she puts the book aside, licks her index finger, and takes the first page from her pile. Her fingers move so rapidly that I can't make out what she's doing. Her mouth is tight with concentration as she watches her moving hands.

A satisfied smile tugs at her lips as she balances a paper bird on her palm. Almost reverently, she sets it on the floor beside her and picks up a new page. I watch as her swift fingers make a mouse, a turtle, a snail, a dragonfly...

Something about the paper animals makes my stomach contract. A weight presses on my shoulders, and I bite my cheek.

I miss beautiful things. I miss color—the red of the setting sun, the green of the buds on the trees, the blue of the river behind our house. In here, everything is gray or brown—dark, as if the Guard has made every effort to remind us of where we are.

And then there's Nora—fourteen years old—the youngest and smallest of us, who can find beauty in here anyway.

I rub the tears from my eyes. The crowd of animals around Nora has multiplied. Smiling, she gets up and makes a pouch out of the bottom of her sweater. She transfers the animals into her makeshift carrier, one by one, and heads toward the showers. There, she sets them atop the low wall separating the corridor from the rest of the Hangar. She fusses over each animal, turning them this way and that until she's satisfied, before stepping back to admire her display. For a moment, the Hangar feels a little more beautiful.

I close my eyes and see my dad before me, deep in thought as he wishes me goodnight from his chair. "You're never too small to do the right thing, Sin," he says. "You're never too small to make a difference. Just look at the bee. Such a tiny creature and yet it has a huge impact on the world. Without bees, there would be no life."

Suddenly, a roar comes from the shower room. Milou bursts out with great strides and, with a swipe of her arm, knocks the paper animals off the wall. She smiles at Nora as she tramples the little turtle, which now lies, crumpled, in a puddle of shower water.

"I don't want to see that stupid mess in *our* space."

With a wild cry, the timid Nora throws herself at Milou like a Tasmanian devil. She's nearly a foot shorter than Milou, but her arms and legs mill at full speed.

"Stay away from my zoo!" Tears roll down her cheeks, and her wristband-wearing arm jerks uncontrollably. "Keep your *filthy* hands off my zoo!"

Milou growls and shoves Nora.

The smaller girl falls to the ground but immediately scrambles back to her feet.

"They're mine! Mine! *Mine!*" Again, Nora throws herself at Milou, hitting and kicking, her face contorted in rage. The other girls run over to interfere, and I join in an impulse. Q and Frankie are right behind me.

Milou exhales sharply through her nose and tries to throw the young girl down again. Unlike last time, Nora sees it coming. She holds her ground and charges at Milou. Everyone's yelling at them now, and the cries morph into the incoherent blur.

I look around. *Where's Rhea?*

Milou howls in agony when Nora grabs her short hair and hangs on it with all her weight. She tries to push Nora away, but she continues to cling to her hair. Milou's arm jerks, but with her free hand, she grabs Nora's palm and sinks her teeth into it.

Nora shrieks and lets go. Milou takes a step back.

They've put each other in check.

I let out the breath I was holding. *Is it over?*

Milou breathes in and out deeply, slipping her hand under her shirt. "You've really gone too far this time. *No one* touches my hair." She plucks a toothbrush held by the elastic band of her sweatpants. The bottom part looks strange—narrower than normal. Too late, I realize that Milou has sharpened the end into a shiv.

Nora tries to retreat into the shower room, but she slips on the puddle of water with her flattened origami turtle still in it. Milou grips the toothbrush like it's a dagger, her face contorting in pain from the shocks of her wristband.

With a deep breath, Milou fights through the pain and crouches down.

Nora rolls away right before Milou can stab her.

Girls start screaming and pushing each other aside to get a better look at the fight in the corridor.

Milou curses, but a smile touches her lips when she looks around, realizing that she's blocking the shower room's only exit.

"You have nowhere to run to, little girl."

Fear flashes across Nora's face as Milou creeps toward her.

The shouting stops. Everyone is holding their breath.

Nora scrambles to her feet, her fear replaced by an angry resignation. "Come on, then. I'm not afraid of you. I'm not afraid of anyone at all."

For a moment, I see the girl she must have been outside the Hangar. Someone who has always had to fight.

I see myself.

"You're wrong." Milou dives onto Nora and slashes the toothbrush across her arm.

A red welt appears, and Nora screams.

"You're not afraid *yet*," Milou finishes. Her eyes darken, and again, she attacks.

"No!" I shout, dashing forward and landing a punch. My body moved on its own.

My blow throws Milou's balance. She rolls off Nora, and I force my weight onto her. When she tries to stab me with her makeshift knife, I shift my weight onto her arm, pinning it down.

My advantage doesn't last long—Milou's other hand shoves me away, and I find myself tumbling into a shower cubicle.

I rise as quickly as possible. We're both back on our feet.

"What's going on?" Rhea steps out of a cubicle, her hair dripping wet. Milou and Nora don't seem to notice her.

Milou turns her back on me, her gaze fixed on Nora again. *She* is the target—not me.

I jump to grab Milou, but before I can, she steps forward, her free hand clamping around Nora's neck. She moves the shiv backward—ready to strike, right into Nora's throat.

The fear of death flashes across Nora's eyes before her arm whips up and her eyes roll back.

As Milou brings the shiv down, Q throws herself forward and shoves Nora out of the way.

"Stop!" Rhea's voice echoes through the Hangar, but she's too late.

The sharpened toothbrush slashes right through the leather of Q's wristband. The device tumbles to the floor at the same moment Nora falls.

Girls gasp as Q dives, scraping her nails across the concrete floor in a desperate attempt to retrieve her wristband. Frankie's hand closes around my arm, and she pulls me back.

Shockwaves travel through my forearm as I watch Q shakily push the device against her wrist. Tears roll down her cheeks as she tries to make it detect her heartbeat. The wristband keeps flashing relentlessly.

Faster.

And faster.

And faster.

For one last time, the numbers flash—and then the screen goes black.

Rhea steps forward. For just a fraction of a second, I see sadness in her eyes. But just as quickly, it vanishes.

"We're out of here." She grabs Milou's arm and pulls her along. "You can't fight someone who's already dead."

TWELVE
132,896

I am stunned, rooted in place. The Long-Termers went back to their beds, taking with them the hulking tension. Now, only emptiness remains.

A hand grabs my arm, and I dazedly look up.

Frankie's face is strained. "Come on, we have to get Nora back to her mattress." She tugs at me while I just stand there. "There's nothing we can do for Q. Not now."

She's right, so I help her carry Nora back to our sleeping area.

Mia keeps asking questions, but I ignore her and crawl deep under my blankets. Images run through my mind like a movie reel. Q was only trying to help, and now she's paying the price. Without a working wristband, there's no way out for her. At least, no way that leads to freedom.

Unless I manage to escape...

I push the idea aside. The more people who know about my plan, the riskier it'll be.

"What now?" I ask Frankie.

She looks at me in despair. "Nothing."

"What do you mean, *nothing*?" I sit up quickly. "Surely there's *something* we can do."

"What do you suggest? Offer her *your* wristband? You saw how quickly it turned off once it no longer detected a heartbeat." Frankie sighs. "Q will need to decide how to handle this herself."

I swallow the sour taste in my mouth as the full meaning of Rhea's words sink in: *"You can't fight someone who's already dead."*

From the moment the wristband stopped registering a heartbeat, Q became dead to the outside world. Her parents will receive the dreaded, black envelope—the official letter stating that Q couldn't handle REZO. They will mourn her, perhaps even hold a memorial service.

And all this time, they won't know that their daughter is still alive.

"But there must be *some* way to let the Guard know!" I exclaim. "We could tell them something went wrong with her wristband. We could send a note along with the next batch of phones. And if we don't deliver a dead body in the switch cell, surely they'll come and investigate, right?"

Mia rolls her eyes. "As if the Guard cares. If they did, they'd have made our wristband straps a lot sturdier. Q isn't the first person this happened to. Apparently, there was a time when cutting off each other's wristbands was as normal as taking each other's mattresses. The Long-Termers used to steal the Guppies' wristbands and put them on. No one ever succeeded in tricking the system, but the attempts became increasingly violent, and it cost several girls their lives. All for nothing." She winces and leans back against the wall. "I heard it was Rhea who put an end to that. She's the one who brought a little peace to the Hangar. I mean, we're not in paradise, but it could be *so* much worse. If the stories are true, our current fights are nothing compared to what came before. No one was brave enough to even shower, and girls went to the bathroom in groups... You were too vulnerable alone."

I wonder what Vallance thinks of such a violent environment. Does he view deaths in the Hangar as acceptable collateral damage?

"We are on our own. Outside, no one cares." Frankie's voice trembles as she utters the words. She rises and walks away.

My eyes follow Frankie as she fetches Q, throwing an arm around her and luring her toward the mattresses. Nothing is left of the cheerful and confident Q I've come to know. Her shoulders are slumped and her eyes are hollow.

I know all too well what it's like to lose yourself.

I try to push away the helpless feeling inside me, focusing on my breathing and relaxing my fists. I watch as the crescent-shaped indents in my palms slowly fade.

Frankie and Q sit beside me.

"Is there anything I can do for you?" I ask.

Q shakes her head. "I don't want you guys to do anything."

"You don't?" I raise my brows. "I don't get it."

"No. Just stay put. Following Rhea's rules is the only way to be safe here, for *you* to be safe here. I don't want—"

"Safe?" My voice cracks. "It's not safe here at all—Frankie's fingers got jammed in a cabinet, Lynn got a *beating* as her goodbye, and Nora got slit with a shiv for trying to decorate the Hangar. None of them did anything wrong." I take a deep breath, fending off tears. "And you... all you did was protect a friend."

Q's face crumples, but I can't stop myself.

"You will never be free again," I continued. "And for *what*?"

Frankie sighs. "That's not—"

"No." I interrupt, consequences be damned. "Q did what each of us should have done—we should protect each other in here. We should stand up for ourselves *and* each other!"

Q's tears have finally dried, and I see a new light in her eyes.

Frankie, her arm still wrapped around Q, grips her even tighter.

Is the newfound resolve I see in them real, or is it just my wishful thinking?

Mia's eyes dart between Q and me. "Neither of you have seen Rhea in action. Milou is just her lapdog—her bark is worse than her bite. But Rhea is *tougher*. She's a fight you can't win."

"Those who aren't strong have to be smart," Frankie replies, backing me up. "I've dealt with tyrants before, and I'm not the type to let them get to me."

Q hesitates and sits up a straighter. "I dunno."

My words seem to have touched something within her. "I'm not saying we should be the ones picking the fights. But we need to stick up for each other when necessary."

"You're all off your rockers." Mia shakes her head. "Come on." She slowly gets up and grabs Q's arm. "I stink, and I need you to support me on my way to the shower."

The two girls walk away, leaving Frankie and me alone on the mattress. She looks at me intensely, and my cheeks run hot.

An open letter to the Ministry of Health

From your correspondent Roger Vallance

Dear Minister,

The Netherlands is in crisis mode. I have no doubt you have picked up on the discontentment among our population. It is only a matter of time before unrest boils over with consequences beyond our control. You now face the most urgent task of your career—turning the tide before it's too late.

After analyzing our research, we believe your most urgent task is to solve the shortage of staff in elderly care facilities and the resulting incidents of residents sometimes going days without a shower or being forgotten at mealtimes.

We would like to present three proposals to address this state of emergency:

1. **Reintroduce conscription:** Not to fight in wars that don't concern us, but for social service. English is now the dominant language in virtually all international relations. By removing useless languages such as German, French, Spanish, Greek, and Latin from our school curriculum in the Netherlands, we can free up time for high school juniors and seniors to serve as interns at elderly care facilities for one day per week. They can take over a substantial amount of caregiver tasks, reducing the weight on our workforce and benefiting the well-being of our elderly.

2. **Reduce welfare benefits:** Far too many people in the Netherlands sit at home without work, waiting for food stamps, and the cost of this keeps rising. This situation is unsustainable. It is the fault of our previous governments that these people were not reintroduced into the labor market. It is a disgrace if social benefits are higher than the minimum salary, and working leaves people worse off than staying home. The system needs to be overturned. Welfare benefits must be lowered, and it must be possible for everyone to work. Let healthcare institutions hire welfare recipients for low wages. These low wages will be added on top of their welfare benefits, so working will always be rewarded.

3. **Strip prisons of their luxuries:** The billions now spent on housing criminals could be better spent elsewhere. No more gyms or internet cafes, no more luxury rooms with televisions. You forfeit your right to privacy the moment you break the law! Assault, theft, and vandalism should not be rewarded. This money should go toward healthcare instead—higher wages and better facilities for those who truly deserve them.

Drastic times call for drastic measures.

To take action, click <u>here</u>!

Sincerely,
Roger Vallance

2.3M likes
298,365 comments
21,034 shares

THIRTEEN
132,864

Frankie's stormy eyes continue to hold mine. "It's not much different in here than it is outside, huh?"

I shake my head.

"Why is it that people are so power-hungry? And why is it always the people who don't have our best interests at heart?"

"I think the best leaders would never choose to lead." I tear my gaze from hers and stare at my socks. "People who *want* to lead only do so to achieve their own agendas."

"I thought it would be different in here. It *seemed* different—at first." Frankie's gaze bores into me, and again, I see the flecks of gray in her eyes. "You stood up for me in the kitchen, even though you didn't know me at the time. That says something about a person's character." She places a gentle hand on mine.

I smile, and the warmth of her palm makes my stomach do weird things. "Well, I don't know if that's always the case, but I just can't stand injustice."

"Everyone should have the chance to be who they are. I'm sure my life would be different if that was the case, but in here, no one can stop us. In here, we can do as we please. In here..."

Frankie's voice trails off, and her thoughts seem to wander.

We sit in silence, her hand on mine—until Mia and Q return. That's when Frankie pulls her arm away. My fingers feel cold without her touch.

"I don't understand why everyone lets Rhea boss them around," I blurt out.

Q sighs. "It's easier to go along with her shit. I never wanted to fight anyone. I wanted to bide my time and get out with as little attention as possible."

I bite my lower lip. "I didn't mean it, you know. What I said about you never getting out. There has to be a way. What if you get into the switch cell with Mia, once her time comes? Without a wristband, you won't get an electric shock, so they won't see you until you're already outside and you can explain what happened—your time would be almost up as well."

"No." Frankie shakes her head, giving Q a sideways glance. "Tampering with the wristbands is a serious crime, even if you're not the one who did it. Stepping outside without a wristband is a one-way ticket to the Drain. No one in the Guard will even hear you out."

"How do you know that for certain?" I ask.

Frankie's shoulders tense up, and her face turns to stone. "My dad," she mutters.

An uneasy silence hangs between us until the door to the yard slides open, calling us to get fresh air. Each day it opens, I dig a little deeper. It's a slow process. Too slow. The others might have realized what I'm doing, but no one has said anything yet.

We all rise.

"I'll be right there," Frankie says. "Just gotta do something first." She squeezes my forearm, and a small shock travels through my wrist.

I nod and walk out, following the others.

As soon as I step outside, I sit next to my pit. The wind has blown some sand into it, but the hole is already five inches deep. I've been at it for over a week now. How long will this take me? Will I be able to escape in time to help Cross?

Without a word, Q sits on the other side of my hole and starts digging too.

I shoot her a questioning look, but she avoids my gaze. The loss of her wristband must have made her more open to alternative solutions.

It's nothing special, but it feels good to be outside—to breathe fresh air and get away from the roar of the air conditioner, even though it keeps the

Hangar from turning into an oven.

As I dig, my mind flashes to Cross.

"Sin, what does grass feel like?" my brother asked once. He sat on his knees in front of our apartment window, pulling back the drapes just enough to study the green field across the street. Even though we live on the seventh floor, Dad hung opaque curtains—just in case someone, somewhere, might catch a glimpse of Cross.

"When you have shoes on, you don't really feel a difference between walking on sand or stone. I guess it's a little softer." I didn't answer his question right —I was too distracted when I replied. I still had homework to finish, including a report to write on the rise of the Netherlands, which I'd been procrastinating on for too long.

"I'm talking about grass, Sin." Cross caught my attention again. *"What does it feel like when you're barefoot? Or when you touch it with your hands? Does it tickle? I bet it tickles. And that it smells nice. Do you know that green is my favorite color?"*

I nodded absently.

"That's my dream. To feel and smell grass someday," Cross continued. *"Once I'm grown up, I'm sure I'll get to go outside."*

Only then did I finally look up from my homework to see the longing in his eyes.

That stupid report could wait a little longer.

"Wait here." I put on my shoes and hurried down seven flights of stairs, running onto the lawn and glancing up. I saw the curtains move, but Cross stayed out of sight.

Using just my hands, I dug up a patch of grass with a clump of soil clinging to the roots. Then, cautiously, I walked back up with a palm full of earth.

I will never forget the look in Cross's eyes when he realized what I'd done. He played with the grass for days until it completely withered and our dad threw it away.

I open my eyes to see Q digging furiously. Frankie still hasn't come out.

I ignore my disappointment and grab another fistful of sand.

Humans aren't hardwired to be locked up.

FOURTEEN
132,596

When I wake, the Hangar is pitch black. Nora, Mia, and Frankie are asleep, but Q's eyes are wide open.

"Six, four, six…"

I turn over to face her, and Q shoots me a startled look. "Oh, did I wake you?" she whispers, pushing herself upright.

"No. I think my brain just figured I'd had enough sleep. Or maybe those stupid daylight lamps are set wrong—night always comes too early for me. Same with mornings. Why are *you* awake?"

"My brain was already switched on too. For the last two and a half months, all I've cared about is serving my time and getting out." Q is silent for a moment. "Now I just feel empty."

"I get it." I look around at the nearby mattresses, ensuring the girls are asleep. Q's honesty makes me want to share a piece of my story with her, but I don't want the others to hear. "The first couple days in here, I felt empty too. At home, I'm used to taking care of Cross, my little brother, but here, that's no longer needed."

I don't notice any disapproval on Q's face when she realizes my parents didn't follow the One Child Policy. It's mostly surprise that I see in her eyes.

"I'm glad you have something useful to return to." She smiles. "Promise me you won't risk that for a vendetta against Rhea and Milou. It won't get my wristband back. You only stand to lose more."

"I know. But I'm used to fighting, even when I can't win." In my mind, I see my dad before me. How many times did he have to tell me that a lone, little chick can't stand up to a pack of wolves?

I push the thought away and focus on Q. Besides helping me dig, she seems to have fully accepted the cruel fate she might face.

"How do you always stay so calm?" I ask.

She shrugs. "How much have you heard about me from Mia, Nora, and Lynn?"

"Nothing, really. I don't really talk with them alone."

Q sighs. "I know there's a lot wrong on the outside, but some things have gotten better. There's more freedom to be who you are, and love who you love, than ever before."

I know she's right, and yet it still stings. If you play by the rules as a valuable member of society—in the eyes of the government, at least—a lot is possible. No other administration has ever called out inequality by race, religion, or gender so openly. Universal basic income solves plenty of other problems too—people can't blame poverty on any one group anymore. But it doesn't make things easier for those who, for whatever reason, are *not* seen as valuable.

Everyone is included. That was Vallance's campaign slogan during the election.

"But even if the government supports you, that doesn't mean your family will." Q breaks the silence with a trembling voice, her hands balling into fists. "My parents are *old school* and want to keep things the way they were before. Marriage must be a union between a man and a woman, there will be no eating during daylight hours at Lent, there should be Bible lessons in public schools..." Q sighs. "Government rules didn't apply within the walls of our home."

Tears well up in her eyes, and her knuckles turn white. I cover her hand with mine.

"I tried to tell them. I wanted to explain how I felt, how tired I was of pretending. But I couldn't. My parents would never have accepted me as Q. I'm..." She turns her face and wipes away tears with her sleeve. "To my parents, I will always be their son. Nothing I say or do will ever change that."

She swallows several times. "But eventually, pretending didn't work anymore. I was so unhappy in my body that I *had* to tell them the truth. And I'll never forget the anger in my father's eyes, and the sadness in my mother's. I packed my things and left that night. I almost asked to stay at a Children's Facility, but I'm sure my parents would have found a way to reclaim me." Q sighs. "So I lived on the streets for a few months instead. I was under eighteen, so I didn't qualify for basic income or housing."

I can't imagine what that must have been like. A few years after the introduction of basic income, homelessness became illegal. If money, jobs, and housing were available to all, why should law-abiding citizens be bothered by people living on the streets?

"Those were the happiest weeks of my life," she adds.

Her words make my head spin.

"I know it sounds crazy. I owned nothing, yet I had more than ever before. I could finally be myself. No more having to meet my parents' expectations, and the demands of their faith. I was *free*. Those weeks gave me the strength to apply for treatment at a gender clinic."

"Then how did you end up here?"

A smile tugs at her lips. "One of the people I met on the street told me about a hidden housing community in the old forts. After sorting out the right papers and stocking up on enough hormones to get by for a while, I decided to travel there. I didn't believe my eyes when I arrived. It was a group of over fifty people."

"*Fifty?*"

"Yes, young and old. All of us chose to live outside the established societal framework. We didn't have basic income, housing, or jobs, but we stuck together. I helped a lot in the vegetable garden. It was nice to use my hands for practical work—very different from my dad's wish for me to spend hours, every day, reading the Bible and writing about it." Q chuckles softly. "Both activities make your hands and back ache, but seeing those home-grown carrots on my plate at dinner time was an extra bonus."

"That sounds great."

"It was." A longing gaze enters her eyes. "But one day, people in suits showed up—people with tablets, notebooks, and measuring equipment. Most people escaped in time, but for the rest of us—the Guard had us pinned within the hour. While they held me down, I watched them trample our vegetable garden. They arrested us for trespassing and vagabonding. We were living in a place forbidden to unauthorized people."

"The new neighborhood." Q's story syncs up with something I overheard once when Dad was watching the news. "Vallance had plans to build a luxury residential neighborhood near one of those forts. Maybe it was yours?"

"Yeah, I figured it was something like that. But what about the other forts? Some of them are from the 1800s. They're not going to demolish *those*, are they?" Disbelief laces Q's voice and her eyebrows draw together into a deep frown. "They'd be destroying our cultural heritage."

"Like Vallance cares. Everything must be improved. Everything must be made new."

"Not everything new is better," Q objects.

"Preaching to the choir, Q."

"So what about you?" She gives me an inquiring look. "How did you end up here?"

I don't hesitate for a moment. She's been so open with me that it feels good to share my story.

"Cross is the sweetest, most wonderful little brother I could ever wish for, but he technically shouldn't have been born. My dad chose not to register him. He always said that our family was exactly as it was meant to be, that there is always enough love for more than one child."

Q grimaces. "My father expected nothing less than perfection from me and my mother. Created in God's image and all that. But your dad sounds like a stand-up guy. I'm guessing you had to hide your little brother, since he wasn't registered?"

I nod. "We kept Cross hidden in our apartment. I took care of him after school until my dad got home from work. I taught him to read. I even made up homework assignments."

"And your mom?"

"Well, before she left us, she worked mostly evening and night shifts.

She stayed with Cross during the day, which was nice. My dad always talked about leaving the country, about moving to a place where we would all feel at home. But it was always just talk—he never took action."

"She left you?"

I gulp hard. "One afternoon, I came home from school to find Cross sitting at the table doing homework I gave him. Without a word, he pointed to the second floor. He always did that whenever Mom went to bed early. It pissed me off when she left him unsupervised like that, so I stormed upstairs, but she wasn't asleep—she was stuffing clothes into a suitcase. When I asked what she was doing, she apologized. Said she couldn't do this anymore. That maybe now, my father would finally learn to put my brother and me before his hatred for the government. Then she clicked the suitcase shut, lifted it off the bed, and headed downstairs. I followed her, confused, and she hugged me. Said she loved me. And then she just... left.

"For a long time, I blamed her. I thought she wasn't strong enough to handle our family. But now I know that leaving took more strength than staying."

Q simply nods, listening intently.

"About a year after my mom left, Cross got sick. Diabetes. I was caught trying to steal insulin."

"And now that you're gone?"

Q asks the very question I've been doing my best to avoid, and it makes my eyes water.

"I always kept some of the stolen insulin as an emergency supply," I explain. But with each day I'm in here, the risk of a hyperglycemia attack increases. If he runs out of insulin, he won't make it—though I don't tell her that part.

"If he's anything like you, he'll figure out how to survive."

I manage a weak smile. Mom always said that Cross and I looked exactly alike, besides our eye color. We have the same light brown hair, the same narrow chin, and both of us are covered in freckles.

Someone shifts behind me, and I startle, glancing over my shoulder. I can barely make out Frankie, pulling the blanket up to cover her shoulders.

I listen intently. Her breathing is regular. She's still asleep.

"I'm glad you're here." Q puts her hand on mine and drops her gaze to my wristband. "But what are you going to do once you get out?"

"I don't know. I can't go back to a life of stealing and secrets. If I get caught again..." I don't have to finish my sentence. We both know what would happen.

"Most of my people managed to get away, remember? I'm sure they're still together somewhere new. What if you could find their new hideout? The doctors might be even able to get you medicine for Cross. I don't know how, exactly, but when one of our people got an infection, we had antibiotics on hand."

"That sounds like a dream." I yawn, and Q laughs.

"Go to sleep. We can talk more later."

With a nod, I turn onto my side and clutch my blanket.

Next to me, Q does the same, and once she closes her eyes, I'm alone with my thoughts again.

A community living off the grid. Would they accept Cross? And me? My chest fills with a longing I haven't felt this strongly before. Perhaps there's a place we can all exist without fear.

FIFTEEN
132,332

I wake up to chattering voices. Q, Nora, Frankie, and Mia sit in a semicircle with trays containing shelf-stable milk and flavorless cereal on their laps.

"Hey, sleepyhead." Q grins at me, a white milk mustache above her lip. "Finally awake?"

"She was probably dreaming about her boyfriend!" Mia shoves a big bite into her mouth, then slides a full bowl toward me. "Frankie got some for you, too."

"Why does it need to be a boyfriend?" Frankie turns to Mia, but I can tell she's watching me out of the corner of her eye. The blood rises to my cheeks.

"Exactly. She could be dreaming about a girlfriend." Q smiles.

"Or a big strawberry milkshake," Nora adds.

"God." Mia rolls her eyes upward. "Why do you guys make such a drama out of every comment? Sin knows what I mean, right?"

"Gee." I get up slowly and walk to the group. "If I had to choose between a boyfriend, a girlfriend, or a strawberry milkshake, that's an easy choice. Although I actually prefer vanilla."

Nora raises her hand and I give her a high five.

"You really don't understand anything at all." Mia crosses her arms and sulks.

Beside her, Q visibly struggles to hold back a laugh. The aggrieved look on Mia's face is the last straw. A jitter bubbles up in my belly, and for the first time in weeks I actually laugh out loud. It doesn't take long for the rest to join in.

We are so absorbed in our laughing fit that I don't notice anything else at first. Only when Nora suddenly stops laughing do I look up. Rhea is staring at our little group from the shower area with a furious look on her face.

Mia shrugs. "Let her glare at us. See if I care."

"We don't know what her life was like before the Hangar." Q talks slowly, weighing each word individually. "Maybe she has a good reason for acting this way. She's just trying to survive, like us."

"No." The word is out of my mouth before I realize it. "You're not seriously going to stand up for her after what she did to you? After what Milou did to you?"

"I honestly don't think that this," Q gestures to her empty wrist, "was their intention." She looks past us and stares into the distance. "If I can let go, you all should be able to as well."

The silence following her statement is almost painful. Part of me knows she is right, but another part is angry—angry that Rhea is taking her frustration out on us, angry that she is hurting others, angry that she has stolen Q's chance at a future. In a reflex, my fists ball up and my heartbeat quickens. A jolt shudders through my arm and I breathe sharply in and out through my nose. I want to say more—shout at them that Rhea and Milou deserve to suffer, that we need to get back at them for everything they've done.

But before I can say anything, Mia, Nora, and Q stand, collecting everyone's empty dishes to take to the kitchen.

Suddenly I am alone with Frankie. She picks at her nails.

"How did you even end up in here?" The question is out before I can hold it back. It's an unwritten rule that we don't ask about each other's pasts, but Frankie doesn't seem to mind.

"I joined demonstrations a little too often. After being at that demonstration against the introduction of the new *one country, one president* legislation, I got a taste for it. But you can only keep showing up for things like that for so long."

I remember the demonstration well. Dad had sat in front of the TV, shouting at the news for a good hour. The law that Vallance wanted to introduce would decrease the frequency of elections. According to him, it was because elections cost too much time and money—money from taxpayers' pockets that would be better spent on healthcare and education. And things were going well, weren't they? Indeed, our country had never thrived like this. We only had to look at the statistics! The food bank was done away with, no more unemployment, and the crime rate had dropped by more than seventy percent in the past five years.

In theory, there was always the possibility of deposing him by referendum, but that possibility was only there in theory, just like demonstrations were still allowed on paper. It was only that civilians who attended the demos were arrested suspiciously often—too often to be a coincidence.

That time was no exception. The news only showed the demonstrations coming to an end: the Guard using tear gas as they rushed the plaza from all sides, grabbing anyone who couldn't get away in time. *Disruption of public order* was the official excuse for breaking up the demonstration. One of the protesters had been found guilty of vandalism, according to the Guard, and the entire group had ignored their call to clear the plaza. What happened to the protesters after their arrest wasn't disclosed, but everyone knew that people who ignore the Guard could only end up in one place.

Frankie sighs. "I don't regret it. I'd do it again in a minute."

Regret. The word keeps bouncing around in my head. Me, I regret every single second I'm stuck in here. I regret not being more careful, I regret letting myself get caught so easily. The only thing I don't regret at all is that I wanted to steal the meds. The very thing that got me sent here, the thing that I have to realize was a mistake, is the one thing that feels absolutely right to me.

"Our president has made a lot of stupid decisions in his life, but the Hangar is the absolute worst." Frankie grabs my arm and tugs me to my feet. "Locking up a group of unsupervised adolescents so they can ponder their sins is doomed to failure. People our age are not exactly known for their rational choices or logical thought processes."

"Are you saying I'm not rational?" I ask, cocking an eyebrow.

"I'm not saying that. You're obviously an exception. You were probably one of those girls who reads books for fun and catches spiders in a cup to take them out of the house without harming them."

I smile. She sees through me so well. "What about you? Are you also full of love for animals and books?"

Frankie looks at me defiantly. "What do *you* think?"

"You want me to answer honestly?"

"Ouch! That doesn't sound like the answer will be very positive." Frankie shakes her head. "But now I want to know."

"I don't know. You just come across as so confident—like you know exactly what you want and exactly how to get it. Usually it's not the super confident types who are into reading."

Frankie smiles. "I learned from books how to act as confidently as possible. At first it was an escape mechanism, a way to get away from my awkward situation at home. But reading taught me how to twist the truth and bend it to my will. How to make sure people saw me the way I *wanted* them to perceive me. Fortunately, I have always been good at judging people and situations. The things I learned from books, I applied to reality. But here, I don't want to do that anymore. Here, I want to really get to *know* people. I really want to get to know *you*, and I want you to see the real Frankie."

SIXTEEN
127,943

Frankie and I sit on my mattress with our backs pressed against the wall.

With a smile, I watch Nora and Q as they do handstands in the corner of our sleeping area. Nora is close to the wall with her legs wide as Q kicks into the air, bringing her legs between Nora's. By now, Nora is beet-red and drops of sweat are beading on her forehead.

Since our conversation, Frankie does seem determined to get to know me. The questions keep coming: about my favorite foods, hobbies, school, books, books, and more about books. Frankie takes in everything, replying to me just as easily when I bounce the questions back to her.

Again and again I keep expecting painful questions—about my home situation, or why I was arrested—but the moment doesn't come.

"Check it out." Frankie nudges me and nods toward the group of Long-Termers. I follow her gaze and see Lindsay take a startled step back, away from Rhea.

"I think Rhea woke up in a funk again this morning. Lindsay didn't do anything—she just grabbed her shoulder and Rhea immediately snapped at her."

"It must be that time of the month," Mia says as she plops down between us. "Hey, scooch—my fat ass can't fit between you two like this."

Frankie rolls her eyes. "You could have *not* wedged yourself between us, you know."

"True." Mia grins broadly. "But where's the fun in that?"

'You have strange ideas about what's fun." Frankie sighs. "But I think it would be wise to avoid Rhea for the time being."

"Boring!" Mia turns and lies down on her stomach, facing us. "I kinda expected you guys to enter in battle. You know: one for all, and Sin and Frankie for justice or something."

"Trust me, if I thought it could help us, I'd fight her. But I've fought before and I know the consequences." Frankie runs her hand across her lower back. "We won't see the end of it. We fight Rhea, and then what?"

"Then the Long-Termers will want revenge," I add.

Frankie sighs. "Exactly. It's a never-ending cycle. An eye for an eye, a tooth for a tooth, a life for a life, until anger is all that remains and no one remembers what it was all about in the first place."

"Wow, you're a bunch of party-poopers all right." Mia gets to her feet. "I'm going to see if we can do that handstand trick with three people. Anything's better than listening to you guys whine."

Frankie watches Mia as she walks away from us. "I've thought long and hard about it. About revenge, I mean. Does fighting back automatically make you a bad person? If you have to do something bad to defeat someone worse—does that make you a monster?"

I shrug. I never thought about it like that. I did what I had to do and I did what I couldn't resist doing. "Maybe not, but sometimes people go too far to achieve their goals. I think Vallance is a prime example of that. I mean, you should always consider what you stand to gain or lose, or what others might lose due to your actions. That's where things usually go wrong."

"And if both you and others get something positive out of defeating the monster—is that a good thing?"

"Yeah, but that's precisely the problem." I want nothing more than to stomp the floor in frustration, like a little kid. "People don't *see* what others lose due to their actions. I think everyone just does things because they think those things are right. I'm sure Rhea doesn't see herself as a monster."

"Maybe we're looking at it wrong. What if Rhea isn't the biggest monster at all?" A burning light flares up in Frankie's eyes. "Isn't the real monster the one who locked us all in here? A monster who locks up his own children with no supervision, no education, no help, no future... Isn't that what we have to fight against?"

Her words sound logical, but in real life, doing that is impossible. How do you fight a government oppressing you, especially when the majority of the population blindly support it? "We *can't* fight, and you just said so yourself: taking revenge is not the solution."

"What's not the solution?" Q looks at us inquiringly as she approaches, Nora and Mia in tow.

"Fighting," I reply.

"Some things are worth fighting for." Q looks at me intensely. "But in here, that's not always obvious anymore."

Nora lets out a deep sigh. "To me, things are just clearer in here." She grabs Q's hand. "You're worth it. You're all worth it, as far as I'm concerned." She looks at us one by one.

"You're worth it too." Q puts her hand on Nora's shoulder and whispers something in her ear.

"What do *you* think is worth fighting for?" As if nothing happened, Frankie continues with her line of questioning.

I see Cross in my mind's eye. His blond spiky hair behind the window —glass that might as well have been made of steel, because he was never allowed on the other side of it.

Perhaps only now do I realize what an impact always being locked inside must have on Cross. Sure, he's not used to it being different, but I often saw him looking out longingly when Dad or I went outside. A painful pang of guilt pierces my stomach. Our house is as much a prison as this Hangar.

Frankie looks at me inquisitively, waiting for my response to her question.

I bite my lower lip before replying.

"Freedom."

SEVENTEEN
122,854

I'm standing in my hole, digging deeper and deeper alongside the steel plate that reaches far into the earth. At some point there must be an end to this thing. Somewhere down there, the plate will end.

By now everyone knows what Q and I are doing, but aside from a few eye-rolls from Mia and Lindsay, no one has commented on it.

The sun is high in the sky and sand and sweat are stinging my back and arms. I've only been here for two weeks, even though it feels like much longer. I've only known Frankie for a week, yet she already means more to me than I care to admit. Our conversations sometimes still feel like interviews, but looking forward to our moments together helps me get through the days. Time moves faster that way. Q, Nora, and Mia also won an important piece of my heart, but with Frankie, it's different. It feels like more.

I push the thought away. As soon as I get deep enough, I'll be out of here. Cross is my priority. I push my fingers into the sand again, but this time they touch something sturdy.

I rub away the sand. More and more sand. And with each piece of the hard object that becomes visible, my heart sinks further. Beneath the sand, the steel plate just runs on. We are in a container. A huge container, filled with sand and surrounded by steel.

Tears well up in my eyes. I'll never get to Cross in time. With clenched fists and wet cheeks, I pull myself out of the hole and storm inside.

I stand in the shower for an endless amount of time, and only when I am completely cold and my fingertips are wrinkled from the water do I put my clothes back on. I get into bed without saying anything to the others.

Hours later, when the Hangar is shrouded in silence and darkness once more, I am still lying awake. My thoughts go in all directions: to Dad, to my home, and to Cross. Mostly to Cross. But in between those thoughts, I also think of Frankie. She hasn't asked me any questions since last night, even when she saw I'd been crying. What if she's lost interest in me? What if she starts spending her time with Nora or Q instead? A stab of pain lances through me.

With a sigh, I turn onto my side and look straight into Frankie's wide-open eyes. Her mattress is right next to mine and if I were to extend my arm, I could touch her right now. I bite my lower lip as I try to push away the urge to do exactly that.

"Can't sleep either?" With a smile, she partly sits up and leans her head on her hand.

"No. I'm mulling things over too much."

"Like what?"

Her penetrating gaze makes me blush.

"Ooh, now I definitely want to know!"

I sigh, because surely I can't tell her the full truth. How can I tell her about Cross... or that *she* was the one I was thinking about besides him? "I was thinking about my useless hole."

Realization dawns on Frankie's face. "About the steel plate."

I nod. "Perhaps I should have known. They would never be so careless. I can't have been the first one to try."

"You had hope." Frankie puts her hand on my arm. "And no one can blame you for that. Hope is necessary to survive in a place like this."

Her words play through my head. It's not about whether *I* survive. It's about Cross. If I don't get out of here soon, he won't. I've been here for over two weeks now. His time is running out."

"You can't give up hope." Frankie's fingers stroke my arm and warm tingles dart across my skin.

She probably doesn't realize how much her words mean to me. I smile. "Looks like you've run out of questions."

"Huh?"

"You haven't asked me anything all day. I'm afraid your interest in me has run out." I am far too aware of the hairs on my legs and under my armpits, which by now must be almost as long as the hairs on my head. I'm sure all the girls at my old school would look at me in horror if they saw me like this, although they did that even when I could still pay attention to my personal hygiene.

"Nah. I could never lose interest in you. I was afraid you'd get tired of me if I asked too many questions. I've heard quite often that I can be too much." Frankie bites her lower lip. "When I talk to you, it feels like I've known you for much longer. It feels like we're not trapped, at least for a little while."

"That's what it feels like to me too."

"I never had real friends, you know. I didn't fit in at the school I attended. They were all people who either acted out or wanted to butter me up because of my father's high position. No one was genuinely interested in *me*. Not like you."

"At my school, it was all about who had the prettiest shoes or the latest model of jeans, things I couldn't compete in even if I'd wanted to."

"Why not?" Her question rings of genuine interest.

"My dad's a biologist. He worked at the old zoo. When I was about seven years old, a group of elephants had to be moved to a new enclosure and something went wrong. An unexpected sound freaked out the elephants and my dad's leg got stuck under one of them. His lower leg was shattered and he could no longer do the work he loved so much. He was transferred to an office in the city, but my dad wasn't made to sit at a computer. He grew profoundly unhappy. Unfortunately, my mom had accidentally gotten pregnant, so he had to keep doing that job, because he knew the extra costs of a second child—especially without the child allowance." I look at Frankie from under my eyelashes, but she doesn't seem startled by my admission.

"After Cross was born and turned out to be a colicky baby that cried non-stop, it all became too much for my dad. He became increasingly angry at everything and everyone around him, but especially at the system. His working hours were cut in half and suddenly we had to make do with only a little more than a basic income at home."

Basic income had been introduced to fairly distribute the costs of subsidies and social benefits among the population. Money for the people, instead of money for the bureaucracy. It was just that the basic income was barely enough to buy enough food for us. Nothing was left over for new shoes or trendy pants, especially with an extra, secret mouth to feed.

Frankie nods and picks at her sweatpants. "I think my father would have a heart attack if he saw me like this. Status and prestige are incredibly important to him. The outside world had to see us as the perfect little family. When I was young, we had photo shoots every year with color-coordinated outfits. Fucking hated it. The tights were always terribly itchy and the collars of the blouses I had to wear choked the life out of me."

I try to imagine Frankie as a young girl forced to play the perfect daughter, but all I can see is a headstrong child sticking her tongue out at the photographer.

"Most memories I have of my childhood end with sermons and punishments, because I didn't live up to their ideal."

"How can *you* possibly not live up to someone's ideal?" Teasingly, I push her arm out from underneath her head.

Frankie moves closer to me and continues to talk in a slightly lower voice. "How many embarrassing examples do you want? About the one time I was playing soccer in the schoolyard and kicked the ball straight through the principal's window? I was given detention and my father had to come and pick me up from the principal's office. He was so calm when he walked in and remained friendly and polite to the principal throughout the whole conversation. He immediately promised that he'd pay for the damage and organize a fundraiser for a soccer cage in the schoolyard. But I knew he'd drop the friendly facade as soon as we got home."

"But that's not something to be ashamed of, is it? It was just an accident. It could have happened to anyone."

"Sure." Frankie grins. "Well, that's what I told everyone. Or, one time as a toddler, I went on vacation to an island with my mom. They had a really nice petting zoo there. You could ride ponies, cuddle bunnies, and there was a playground. When it was time to go, I refused to come with her. She carried me away from the lambs while I was kicking and punching. Fortunately, my father was on a work visit to the Drain and my mom knew better than to tell him about it."

"Your dad sounds like a tough guy to please." I bite the inside of my cheek and don't let go of her gaze.

A look I haven't seen on Frankie's face yet crosses over it like a shadow. It's like pain, mixed with anger and resentment—*especially* resentment. She nods, then smiles, but the smile doesn't reach her eyes. "We should go to sleep. Before you know it, the lights will come back on." Frankie stretches out her arm and grabs my hand. "I'm glad I can share so much with you."

"Me too. That I can do that with you, I mean."

Frankie continues to hold my hand and ducks deeper under her blankets. "Sleep tight."

"Don't let the bedbugs bite."

Frankie closes her eyes, and within a few minutes, her breathing slows. I try to follow her lead, but her hand burns on mine. Her skin is soft, and her trimmed nails have grown out a little. The bulge of a small scar runs down the back of her hand. Very carefully, I let go of Frankie's hand and put it back on her own mattress. I look at her relaxed face one more time before I lie on my back and wait for sleep to come.

Within seconds, I hear Frankie get up. Apparently she wasn't as deep asleep as I thought. I crack my eyes open, just barely, to see her walk to the restroom.

With eyes closed, I wait for her to return, but she takes too long. I consider getting up to figure out what's going on, but something stops me—the memory of that look on her face when I talked about her father. Maybe she just needs space.

With a sigh, I roll onto my other side. Even when I finally feel myself beginning to slip into a dream, Frankie still hasn't returned.

EIGHTEEN
122,819

"What are you thinking about?" Q's teasing voice snaps me out of my thoughts. "Never mind. I can already guess from that smile on your face. What sweet thing did Frankie tell you this time?"

I can't keep the blood from flooding my cheeks. Since we had that talk the other night, something has changed between us. But even though we have grown closer, both of us avoid the subject of her family.

"That's all I ever do, right?" With a wide grin, Frankie steps out of the shower room. "To Sin, at least."

"Yup. You're not nearly as sweet to me."

Frankie chuckles. "No, but you don't need it. No one is as strong and tough as you."

"True, but I won't say no to you sweet-talking me, you know." Q blows a kiss to Frankie, who pretends to catch it and press it against her heart.

Something in their exchange feels so easy, and at the same time it hurts. Maybe Frankie is just like this with everyone, but for me things are different. I've never felt this way with anyone else—the honest conversations, the brief touches that send tingles through my body, the feeling that I've known her for years...

But what if Frankie feels like that with everyone? A stab of jealousy runs through my heart. Maybe Frankie likes Q more. Maybe I've been seeing things.

"Well then, I'll just ask everyone to leave so I can whisper sweet nothings in your ear," Frankie says, wiggling her eyebrows.

Q and Frankie chuckle. The sound of their laughter awakens an array of repressed memories within me. With all my might I try to push away the unpleasant feelings, but I can't stop the anger flooding back from the past.

I clench my fists, bad thoughts racing through my head. *They don't want me here. They don't need me at all. I'm not needed anywhere.*

"Right. Don't let me stop you." I get up brusquely. "I know when I'm not wanted." I hear how catty and jealous my comment sounds, but I can't stop myself. I don't want to feel this way ever again.

"Where did *that* come from?" Frankie looks at me in surprise and it takes a second for her to realize. "It was just a joke."

Her words trigger me more than I care to admit. All the times I've been left out, all the times I didn't belong...

I hold back tears and walk to the toilets. I have to get out of here. The second I shut the cubicle door, it hits me—wave after wave of memory. I can't stop them. I can't even breathe between them.

I'm back in the dean's office at my old school.

"It was just a joke, sir. I would never intentionally hurt Sin. She's having a hard enough time as it is." Carmen pouts at the dean, blinking those innocent eyes of hers. The bruise under her eye blooms purple, but I don't feel bad. Not even a little. I might even feel a bit *satisfied*.

"This isn't funny," the principal growls, noticing my smile. "I won't tolerate this behavior at my school."

I don't dare look at him, so I lower my gaze. His brown leather shoes gleam under the bright fluorescent lights, and the tips of Carmen's ballet flats are as white as freshly fallen snow—a sharp contrast to my gray, kicked-off sneakers.

He orders me to reflect on what I've done, and though I try not to, I think back to earlier that morning, when I was locking up my shared bike at the school dock.

"Why are you inviting her, anyway?" a girl asked, catching my attention.

I looked over to see Carmen and her friends nearby. They didn't even bother whispering, though they clearly noticed me too.

Carmen leaned into an exaggerated sigh. "My mom always loves a charity project."

"She can't be serious," one of her friends said.

"Better put the nice vases away," teased another. "If someone looks at her funny, she might go feral and start breaking things."

The girls laughed, and I dug my nails into my palm as they made their way toward me.

Without making eye contact, Carmen handed me a light pink envelope. My name was written on it in ornate lettering.

She smiles and whips around. "Cool, I've done my good deed for the day. Let's just hope her crazy dad won't let her go."

The black hole took over again. Before I knew it, I had a fistful of Carmen's hair. I yanked her toward me and punched her—straight in the face.

There's a quiet knock on the door to my toilet stall.

"Sin?" Frankie sounds hesitant. "You know I didn't mean it, right?"

Of course I know it, but all the painful memories are one big tangle. Sometimes it seems like the new people I meet automatically become part of my past—and I expect them to treat me the same way people treated me before. I know if I can pull the right string, it might unravel everything, but that string hides under an awful lot of memories.

Don't trust anyone unless they have proven otherwise, I tell myself, my dad's voice echoing in the motto.

"Sin?"

With a trembling hand, I unlock the door. It's not her fault.

Frankie frowns and grabs my fingers, her thumb rubbing the back of my hand. "I didn't mean to hurt you."

Although everything inside me cries not to, I believe her.

Without letting go, Frankie puts her other hand on my cheek. "Are we good?"

My skin burns. The hairs on the back of my neck stand up and my stomach flutters, but I don't quite dare admit the feeling just yet. I remove her hand from my cheek and nod.

"Great. Now come on—let's talk to Q. I think she's worried." Frankie chuckles. "I had to pull out all the stops to get her to let me see you alone. I think she was about to push me aside and walk over here herself. I don't know if you've noticed, but she's a tad overprotective at times."

Frankie leads me back to our sleeping area, where Nora and Mia have joined us. A little embarrassed, I give Q a slight nod to indicate that everything's okay. She smiles, rests a gentle hand on mine, and continues her conversation with the others.

I have no idea what they're talking about, so I stare at my feet. After a while, the conversation drops off, and everyone sits in silence. The air conditioning in the Hangar is on full blast. It must be nearing the end of spring by now. I hope my dad fixed the air conditioner on time. Last year it suddenly started making weird, sputtery sounds toward the end of summer, and with the temperatures dropping there was no need to fix it right away. But my dad is gone for work during the day. What if he doesn't notice how hot it gets inside? Cross is stuck there all the time.

I try to shake the thought away and shut out the Hangar's air conditioning noise. To distract myself, I look at Frankie. She sits across from me, smiling and talking to the other girls.

Next to me, Q closes her eyes. "I need to catch up on some Zs. The last few nights I couldn't sleep on account of Mia's snoring."

"I *don't* snore!"

"Sure you don't." Q raises a brow. "I swear, you're hiding a power drill under that blanket."

Mia chuckles. "Wouldn't you like to know all the things I've been hiding under my blanket?"

"Yuck." Nora grimaces.

Mia gets up and sashays away. "I'm gonna take a shower."

"Wait!" Nora runs after her. "I'll come with you, as long as you promise not to say anything gross again."

"Geez," Q snorts, then lies on her mattress. "Good night, everybody."

Suddenly Frankie and I are alone again—or at least, the closest you can get to *alone* in the Hangar.

"I..." I want to break the tense silence hanging between us, but the words clot in my throat. I'm painfully aware of how I look with my soggy jogging suit, cropped hair, and bare face. "Sorry about just now."

She squeezes my hand and rests a palm against my neck. Her fingertips caress the stubble on my head, and goosebumps spread across my arms.

Slowly, she pulls me closer, inch by inch, giving me every chance to say no, to pull back.

But I let it happen. I *want* her closer. Right now, there's nothing I want more.

NINETEEN
122,430

Her lips touch mine—gently at first, then more firmly. Her hand slides down to my neck again, and she pulls me closer. I press my upper body against hers and wrap my arms around her shoulders. For once, my mind is completely quiet. No questions, no pondering, just her mouth on mine.

Her hands move from my neck to my waist, leaving a trail of heat across my skin. She wraps her arms around me and pulls me even closer. Slowly she lowers herself onto the mattress, lying on her side and guiding me to her.

As soon as we are side by side, she pulls away from me a little, looking at me up close. Her eyes are big and her breathing is rapid. Her wristband must sting her too, but it's not bad enough to really hurt. Grinning, she looks at my wrist, then back at me.

I force myself to take a few deep breaths before drawing her close. I cup her cheek with one hand. Her skin is soft under my fingertips. When her tongue finds mine, another electric jolt shoots through my wrist.

For the first time since I've been in the Hangar, I want to stop time. If I could, I would keep this moment forever and let our kiss be all there is.

Only when we are both out of breath do we let go of each other. I'm sure the grin on her face is mirrored in mine. We remain still, staring at each other. I don't want to blink, afraid of losing a split second with her. I want to take in every minute detail of her face: her eyes that are almost blue, the dimple in her left cheek when she smiles, the small scar above her eyebrow, her lips... Every time, my gaze goes back to her lips.

This time, it is Frankie who presses her lips to mine. The tingling in my stomach flares up again when she slides her hand from my hip down to my buttocks and lets it rest there.

"Huh?"

Q's voice startles my eyes open. I look over, and she meets my gaze, grinning when she notices my arms wrapped around Frankie. "Oh, finally. I was starting to think you two were never gonna happen."

The blood rises to my cheeks, and I jolt upright. Part of me feels cheated. I knew fully well that we didn't have any privacy—that someone could look our way at any moment—and yet, for just a minute, the world seemed to belong to Frankie and me.

I'm not at all ready for other people to meddle in whatever is going on between us. I don't even know what *this* is. Do I even want it to continue? What would that mean in here, anyway?

"I have to pee." Those are the only words that leave my mouth.

"I was just about to go too." Q gets up and hooks her arm through mine. "I'll bring her back safely," she tells Frankie, who stares ahead, lips swollen.

Once I'm alone in a toilet stall, I think of everything that just happened. Her mouth on mine. Her warm breath against my cheek. It's not my first kiss, but it *is* my first kiss with a girl. The first kiss where the fluttering in my stomach drowns out the fluttering in my head. The first kiss where I actually *like* the person I'm kissing.

I flush and head to the sink to splash some water on my face, hoping it'll force my burning cheeks to return to their usual color.

Q steps out of the other cubicle, and can't suppress a wide grin as she looks at me. "I'm happy for you."

"What for?"

Q's grin only widens. "I'm not deaf, and I'm not blind. I'm glad something positive is happening in this place for once. I like you guys together."

"Thank you. I like us too. I-I like *her*." I stammer over my words. "Even though I have no idea what that means."

Q shrugs. "It means what you want it to."

"I don't know what I want."

That's when Frankie rounds the corner.

"Aaaaand that's my cue to leave." Q squeezes Frankie's shoulder on her way out.

"Did you hear us?" I glance at her, my cheeks hot again.

"I have good ears." Frankie takes my hand. "You'd rather I hadn't?"

"No. Yeah. I don't know."

"I think we should trust that we met for a reason. Whatever is happening is a good thing."

I smile. "Trust isn't really my strong suit."

"Is it anybody's?" Frankie smiles. "But I do think we have to *learn* to trust." For a moment, she falls silent, seemingly lost in thought. Hesitantly, she adds, "Can I show you something?"

"Sure."

Without explanation, Frankie leads me into the shower room. "I don't know if I'm doing the right thing by showing you this, but I want to put my money where my mouth is, and... prove that trust is possible."

"You don't have to prove anything."

"Yeah, I do. Maybe not to you—or not *only* to you. I have to prove it to myself too."

She pulls me along, toward the far wall of the shower room, and comes to a stop in front of the cabinet containing the towels.

Frankie squeezes my hand, lets go, and takes a deep breath. I watch the muscles in her arms and back tighten as she shoves the cabinet aside. With every inch that the cabinet shifts, another part of the wall becomes visible. There's a toothbrush on the floor, the handle filed into a sharp point like a shiv. And above it...

It takes a moment for my eyes to decipher what I'm looking at.

And then, my heart breaks.

Universal basic income is our number one priority!

From your party leader Roger Vallance

As elections draw near, the Party for the People is stepping forward with more of our initiatives. We want to inform you as best we can about the impact you could make if you vote PFTP.

Today we are presenting the most important spearpoint of our campaign: universal basic income for every Dutch citizen.

Enormous sums are lost each year tracking down welfare fraud, along with organizing and paying for housing benefits, child benefits, and healthcare subsidies. Even more money is squandered on what we call Hotel de Penitentiaries—prisons that look more like five-star hotels, funded by your taxes.

A universal basic income—for citizens 18 and up—would eliminate these extra costs. Money would go directly to the people instead of being gobbled up by bureaucracy. This income would cover baseline necessities such as shelter, food, and healthcare. No more young people who can't go to university due to lack of money. No more children who go to school hungry.

With a huge reduction in administrative costs, we will also have more hands in healthcare, more help in classrooms, and more locally produced goods. This will create marvelous employment opportunities to allow spending beyond the basic income—such as for vacations or luxury goods.

By voting Party for the People, you are choosing a healthier Netherlands.

Together we are stronger. Choose PFTP!

For more information or to donate, click here!

5.3M likes
976,442 comments
53,826 shares

TWENTY
121,787

The entire wall is covered in scratches. As I stare, they morph into coherent images—both beautiful and terrible.

While the drawings are scraped into the wall, the details are stunning. My eyes dart between each scene: a little girl hugging herself, and a man towering over her with a belt. A slightly older girl, arms spread wide in front of a crying woman. A girl about ten years old, blocking the man's belt with her forearm.

"He wasn't happy about that. It's how I got this one." Frankie rubs the scar on her arm. "These kinds of marks weren't as easy to hide as the ones on my back."

"Is that..." I hesitate, staring back at the drawings. "Is that your dad?"

"Yes."

"And no one ever helped you?"

"No one *knew*. Well, my mom must have, but she couldn't stand up to him. Never did." Frankie's voice trembles. "And my father's close friend, Jonathan Hawking—he knew."

Something flickers in the back of my mind when she mentions that name. I'm sure I've heard it before, but I can't remember where.

"He walked in about three years ago, while my father was doling out my corporal punishment," Frankie continues. "I remember looking up at Jonathan while I was crying, welts on my bare back, hoping he would help me. But he just smiled at my father. 'I see you have everything fully under control at home, just the rest of the country.' Then he said the car was ready, and that he'd be waiting for my father outside."

"I'm so sorry." It's the only thing I can manage to say. I put my arm around her, suddenly afraid of touching her back.

"I never really understand why people apologize for something they have no control over." Frankie sighs. "I did that myself for a very long time, you know. I held myself responsible for something that wasn't my fault. I thought it *was* my fault, that I wasn't good enough... that if only I was a little bit smarter, or behaved better, or was more polite, I would be. But by taking the blame, I exonerated *him*. And I refuse to do that any longer. There is only one person responsible for what happened in my home, and that's my father."

What she said on her first day here finally clicks: *"I knew that sooner or later, I'd end up in the Hangar..."* Seeing these drawings, I realize that for some people, their time in the Hangar might be more of a respite than a punishment.

Frankie lowers herself to the floor and looks up at her work. "I was hoping it would help—that I could get it out of my head by drawing it on the wall."

I sit next to her. "Did it?"

"Kinda. I guess it helps to distance myself from it all. I can literally walk away from it, shove that cabinet in front of it whenever I don't want to look. But on the other hand, it's made me angrier, not calmer. I'm no longer mad just for myself, but also for that little girl on the wall. I'm angry for the toddler who didn't know what she did wrong, for the girl who had to wear a long-sleeved shirt on the last day of elementary school in the sweltering heat. For my mother. *At* my mother."

Frankie is silent. Tears well in her eyes.

"She should have protected me, but she never did. And then one day, she was just gone. I mean, her body was still there, but her spirit was gone. My dad broke her. He made her into a passive woman who stands beside him like a Stepford Wife, smiling gently and doing what she's asked. No more, no less. I think he hoped I'd become like that too."

I gaze at the drawings as her words sink in. They hurt. Frankie is so alive, so beautiful, so full of fire. I can't imagine what kind of sick person would want to break that.

"But instead of breaking me, I became even more rebellious. If I was scared because I was running late on my way home from school, I'd stay out instead. I slept at friends' houses, on the street, and once, even behind our toolshed. I'd wait until he had visitors to return home, so he'd have to keep up appearances. Over time, I got to know more people on the street. I got involved in riots against the Guard, against the government. They caught me at a protest while I was spraying graffiti on a poster. Even my father couldn't save me from the Hangar."

Frankie holds out her wristband. Its red numbers are clearly legible: 92,499. "He *did* make sure I got a lighter sentence, though. He's probably thinking I'll come back home begging for forgiveness, that I'll be *grateful* I wasn't detained longer." Frankie's face hardens. "But he's wrong. I'll never go back. I'll build my own life without him."

"What about your mom?"

"She died a long time ago. At least it feels that way. I won't be able to save her."

The pain in her voice overshadows her nonchalant words. I know all too well how she feels. I talk about my mom the same way. She chose to leave us, and I chose to pretend I didn't care. And yet, there's a part of me that still thinks I should have stopped her that day—that I should have been a better daughter. But what if there was nothing I could have done to change her mind, even if I tried?

Frankie's finger catches a tear on my cheek. "You're crying."

"Sorry."

"No need to apologize for it."

She doesn't ask, but I still feel the need to explain. "Sometimes I think that my mom leaving was my fault, but I don't think there was anything I could have done about it. I think she made up her mind long before she closed that door."

"I think so too. Everyone is responsible for their own choices."

Without thinking, I wrap my arms around her. "Thank you. For everything you do for me."

After a moment, Frankie sighs and stands up. "I like feeling useful." She starts pushing the cabinet back into its former position, covering her work. "I know it's pointless—covering it up with this cabinet. Anyone could just move it again, and some of the other girls have already seen what I've been drawing on at night. But it still feels good to hide it. Makes me feel like I'm in control of something."

"That way you can decide when to face it and when not to." I push myself up from the concrete floor. "It's all in your own hands."

Frankie interlocks her fingers with mine. She pulls me in, and our lips meet. Before I can even think, her palm slips under my shirt to caress the skin of my lower back.

I wrap my arms around her neck and lean my head into hers. I feel her warm breath on my lips like a whisper.

And then Nora screams.

TWENTY-ONE
121,645

I tear away from Frankie and dart from the shower room. I hear her footsteps behind me, but I don't wait for her to catch up. Something's wrong.

In the kitchen, several girls are gathered around something.

I push everyone aside, searching for Nora.

"Stop," Frankie whispers, her hand tightening around my arm.

Then I see her—Nora sits on the floor with her back against the kitchen cabinets, her hand pressed against the side of her head.

Q stands protectively in front of Nora, beads of sweat gathering on her reddened forehead.

Mia hesitantly lingers a little ways away.

Rhea and Milou tower in front of Nora and Q. Rhea's fists are clenched. "No!" she snaps at the two girls across from her.

Lindsay tries to approach from the Long-Termer area.

"You stay out of it!" Rhea barks, and Lindsay halts immediately.

I turn to Mia. "What's going on?"

"I was sitting on my bed—and it all happened so fast. I don't even know what *it* is. Milou's just looking to start a fight."

"I can do whatever the hell I want," Milou says. "I have the right to live here just as much as you do. You're not my boss."

Nora stands and tries to stagger forward, but Q stops her. She moves to keep shielding Nora from Rhea and Milou's reach. "Leave Nora alone.

Whatever fight you want to pick with her, pick it with me instead!"

"And me." I pull away from Frankie's grip and stand next to Q.

"Leave, Sin," Q snaps at me. "You have nothing to do with this."

"Hah." Milou presses her lips together. "So much love for that little bitch. If I have to, I'll take all three of you."

"All four of us." Frankie joins Q and me.

"You're the bitch here, Milou!" Nora tries to shove her way through us, but this time, Mia grabs her by the waist, lifts her up, and carries her to the other side of the kitchen.

Milou and Rhea stand in place, their eyes locked on Frankie, Q, and me.

"You should think twice about who you're picking fights with," Q says. "Because I have absolutely nothing left to lose. All thanks to *you*."

With a strangled cry, Q lunges, and her fist strikes Milou right in the temple.

Milou retaliates, grabbing Q by the ear. They both tangle and crash to the kitchen floor.

"Enough!" Rhea yells. I can tell she's about to join the fight, and black spots dance before my eyes. I don't have much time.

My fingers close around the fabric of Rhea's collar, and I yank her back. The sweater is so tight now she can't breathe. She claws at it with her jagged nails.

The other girls start cheering us on. I glance at Q. She's on top of Milou now, pummeling her face.

In my moment of distraction, Rhea kicks backward, her heel hitting me just below the knee. I yelp, and my leg gives out. It doesn't take long for her shoulder to ram into my chest, and I fall backward, Rhea on top of me. Panting, she presses her forearm to my throat. "I warned you."

I press my lips in a grim line, struggling to stay calm.

As if on cue, Frankie and Mia pull Rhea off me, and the three of us force her to the floor.

Q is still pinning Milou, whose wide eyes dart to Rhea.

"Let go of her," Milou warns. "You don't understand." She struggles to free herself until Q suddenly lets go. Milou topples backward, her head of red hair slamming against the floor. She groans and stays down.

Lindsay's gaze volleys between Rhea and Milou, but she doesn't step in.

I focus on Rhea again, who is still struggling, screaming, and cursing beneath me. Mia and I are holding her arms while Frankie clutches her legs.

To my surprise, tears start rolling down Rhea's cheeks. "Let go of me! Let me the fuck go!" Every muscle in her body tenses. "Please!" Her arm trembles, and a raw, animalistic scream rips from her throat.

Part of me feels sorry for her. I see it in her eyes: the agony, the panic. But another part knows that she could easily strike back.

"We won't let you go until you control yourself." Frankie's voice is quiet, but all the more menacing.

Rhea's breathing quickens as she struggles and screams again—first in anger, then in pain. Her whole body trembles, and her eyes roll back. I gasp and finally let go.

Her limp body sags to the floor, where she lies motionless and pale.

"No!" Milou stands with a groan, stumbling toward Rhea.

Q follows my gaze and nods at Rhea. "It's shock, that's all. She'll wake up in a few minutes."

The other Long-Termers watch us from across the kitchen. Without Milou and Rhea to lead them, they seem to have lost their courage.

"As far as I'm concerned, this ends now." Frankie glares at Milou. "Everyone here has been punished enough already. There's no reason we should make each other's lives any harder."

Milou shakes her head. "You have no idea what's going on here."

"Well I know Nora doesn't have anything to do with it. She's just a kid." Q gestures to Nora, who still has her hand pressed against her head.

"I'm not a kid!" Nora pipes up. Mia shushes her.

"You wouldn't be able to understand, anyway," Milou says.

"Of course not, if no one explains it to us." Q's voice is quiet, the anger gone now.

"It's not my choice to explain."

On the floor, Rhea's muscles stiffen, and she jerks around wildly, gasping for breath.

Frankie, Q, and I step toward her on impulse. But Milou nods at us, signaling that she can handle her, and helps Rhea up alone. Two more

Long-Termers show up to help Milou carry Rhea back to their corner of the Hangar.

Once they've left the kitchen, Nora faces us with a hand on her hip. "I could have sorted this out myself, you know."

"I know." Q places a gentle palm on Nora's shoulder. "But we care about you, okay? When you throw yourself at someone two heads taller than you and act like a wild baboon, you shouldn't be surprised if we step in to protect you."

"It's not fair," Nora whines. "Why does Rhea think she's in charge? She needs to learn to shut the hell up!"

Q slips her arm around Nora's waist, and slowly, the younger girl starts to relax. Seeing Q act like an older sister reminds me of Cross, and a pit starts to form in my stomach. I wish there was a way to contact him, if only for a moment. I wish I could find out if he's okay. I wish I could tell him that I still think about him every single day.

Once I get out of here, I'll take him with me. For so long, I've imagined leaving home with him and moving to a place where he could live freely, registered or not. I realize now that we don't have to wait until Dad steps up, or the two of us grow up. We can take action now.

I refuse to leave Cross locked up in that house any longer. He'll be happier outside.

Maybe I will too.

TWENTY-TWO
110,402

We walk on eggshells for days after the fight. Rhea only shows herself when she needs to use the toilet, and even then, she's always with another Long-Termer at her side. I haven't heard her voice in days, and the circles under her eyes have darkened.

By now, everyone knows that me and Frankie are a thing, but fortunately, no one's been asking questions I don't have answers for. Everyone is far too busy with their own problems.

The switch cell's beeping reverberates through the Hangar. New supplies are in.

Milou, Lindsay, and another Long-Termer clear out the switch cell at lightning speed.

Mia and Frankie rise to swap out our crate of disassembled phones with the new one, but Milou and Lindsay block the entrance with their arms crossed.

"What are you doing?" Mia asks. "Get out of the way. This isn't a game."

Milou and Lindsay remain silent, feet planted firmly.

"Come on, Milou." Frankie sets the crate on the floor and raises her palms in surrender. "You'll be punished too if you stop us from doing our jobs. Just let us swap out the crates."

I scan the Long-Termer section—they haven't taken this week's food to the kitchen, but to their own sleeping area. This is their revenge for what happened to Rhea.

They can't do this. They can't let us starve.

Mia's shoulders go stiff when she realizes what they're planning. "You retarded *bitches.*"

Frankie puts her hand on Mia's arm, warning her to cool down.

"You only have yourselves to blame for this." Milou slams the switch cell door shut, hiding the crate of new phones from view.

Less than an hour later, the Hangar's lights dim. I can make out my feet, but nothing else.

Mia sighs. "Typical."

"Huh?" I ask.

"Our punishment. We didn't meet last week's phone quota, so the Guard's cutting off everything: food, light, fresh air... Listen."

I listen, and sure enough, it's silent. Dead silent. "The AC is off."

"Yup. And you may like the quiet now, but in a few hours, you'll be sweating out of your nostrils. And if you think the yard will provide relief, you're wrong. That door will stay shut for at least a week."

"You're kidding." I frown at her. "That's torture."

"A very effective torture, honestly. This is the first time in *eighty days* that we haven't made our quota."

Five days pass. The hunger, heat, and silence are making us all dwell on the consequences of our actions—both within and outside of these walls that bind us.

Yesterday, as well as this morning, the Long-Termers have finally been leaving us food on the kitchen counters. But it's not even enough to satisfy a single person. There isn't a single minute in the day where I don't hear my stomach grumble.

"Why didn't more people rebel when Vallance amended the law?" Q leans against the cool stone wall in an effort to combat the heat. Sweat beads form on her upper lip and forehead. Like the rest of us, she's only wearing a bra and a pair of rolled-up sweatpants. "There used to be elections every four years, sometimes more. But now Vallance has been in power for *fifteen years*. People don't even think for themselves anymore."

"Of course they do, but they're afraid." Frankie stares blankly at the walls. "You know what happens to dissenters, right?"

I sigh. "The Guard can *always* find a reason to arrest people."

I know how our president's speeches always go: *The numbers speak for themselves. No hunger, no poverty, no one living on the streets. The only people against harsh penalties for criminals must be criminals themselves. What other reason could there be?* Yada, yada, yada...

Mia lets out a deep, exaggerated sigh. "I can't take it anymore. Everyone is too gloomy right now. In less than ten thousand minutes, I'll be out of here. I can't leave you guys like this, can I?"

"You could also stay," Q teases. "Snug as a bug, together with all of us, until the end of time."

"I'm afraid I'll have to decline. But I do have an idea to make my farewell a memorable one. Your birthday's coming up soon, right?"

"Um, no?" Q looks at Mia in surprise. "My birthday's in winter."

"Your half-birthday then. I say that calls for a party. If you squint in this dim light, it kinda looks like a club in here, doesn't it? Without the music, dancing, and drinks, of course."

"You really are crazy." Q shakes her head.

"Pleasantly disturbed, I like to call it, with the emphasis on *pleasant*." Mia turns her head toward the shower room, which Nora is just leaving. "Nora! We're celebrating Q's birthday tonight!"

Nora looks puzzled. "A birthday party?"

Frankie shrugs. "Mia's trying to cheer us up, and maybe it's not such a bad idea. In two days, our punishment will probably be over, and the new shipment of food will arrive, and the AC will kick in again. We can't let ourselves be bullied into submission. Let's show the Long-Termers what true friendship can do."

Nora smiles from ear to ear and skips to her mattress. "I don't have a present prepared yet, but I'm in."

"Okay, it's settled then." Mia checks her wristband. "We'll start in... 100 minutes. That'll give you enough time to come up with a smashing performance for the open mic."

Q's eyebrows draw together in a frown. "Open *what*?"

"They used to do that kind of thing at the end of the term, back when school was still fun. My father used to tell me about it. 'Singing, dancing, stand-up comedy, anything goes,' he'd say. It was one of his favorite things." Mia smiles. "When I was little, I'd ask him to tell me about open mic nights instead of reading the boring children's books about the rise of the Netherlands that my mom would bring home from the library."

"Sounds like fun." Frankie grabs my hand. "We'll sing a duet."

I don't reply. Honestly, I don't want to sing at all. I can't carry a tune.

"Either *Summer Nights* from Grease or *Paradise by the Dashboard Light* by Meat Loaf and Ellen Fowley. You get to choose!" Frankie doesn't seem to notice my hesitation—or deliberately chooses to ignore it—but the effect it has on Mia remains the same. She's beaming.

Exactly 100 minutes later, Mia has moved all the mattresses to form a semicircle.

"Ta-da!" She proudly gestures at them. "Our arena, where we will all compete for one thing: to win the honorific title of *Best Act at Q's Half Birthday*."

"Cool!" Nora runs to her mattress and plops onto it.

"Distinguished guests, welcome to Q's spectacular half-birthday spectacle." Mia points to the crate of disassembled phones in the middle of the semicircle. "Birthday girl, this is your throne for tonight."

Nora and Frankie clap as Q reluctantly sits on the crate.

"See, that's the enthusiasm I am looking for!" Mia bows. "And now, ladies, it's time for the first act. Frankie and Sin are going to sing for us!"

Frankie and I line up in front of Q. Frankie's clear voice rings out, and encouraged by her enthusiasm, I sing along after all. I only know the words to the chorus, but that doesn't seem to bother Frankie. She easily takes care of both parts.

After us, it's Nora's turn. Her sweater is folded tightly in her hands.

In a cross-legged position, she sits down in front of Q. All four of us are quiet as she pulls a stack of paper out of her bundled sweater and begins to fold. I know what's coming, and yet I marvel anyway. Her fingers create paper animals, and she sets them on the floor one by one, in a single file. A monkey, a dog, a crane. Then she gets up and places the animals on Q's lap.

"Congratulations on your half-birthday." Nora kisses Q's cheek. "These are for you. A monkey, because you behave like one from time to time…"

Everyone bursts out laughing.

"A dog, because you're incredibly loyal," Nora continues. "And a crane, because cranes bring love and happiness, just like you."

Q moves the animals to the floor and pulls Nora into a hug. "How sweet!"

"And now it's my turn." Mia stands and winks at Nora, who leaves Q with a giggle. "Saving the best for last!"

I have no clue why Mia put her sweater back on, because it's way too hot in here. She marches right up to Q, looks over at Nora again, and nods —some kind of cue.

Nora starts clapping and motions around for the rest of us to join her.

Applause fills our little circle. Mia puts one hand on Q's shoulder, blowing her a kiss with the other. Then, she slowly circles Q, looping around her a few times before suddenly sitting right on her lap.

Q's face turns bright red. Frankie and Nora start cheering.

Mia runs her hands down Q's back, moving her hips to the beat of our clapping. Then she brings her face forward and lands a kiss on Q's neck.

Slowly, Mia rises to her feet, still moving her hips. She bends forward and lets her hands slide up her own legs. Once she reaches her belly, she grabs the hem of her sweater and pulls it off.

Mia stands in front of Q in just her bra, and behind us, some of the Long-Termers are even cheering her on.

Mia swirls her sweater in the air as she circles Q again. She comes to a stop behind her and uses her sweater to tie Q's hands behind her back.

More cheers.

Once again, Mia lowers herself onto Q's lap, folds her hands around her neck, and bends forward so her breasts are in Q's face. The Long-Termers keep shouting, louder and louder. I look over my shoulder to see them standing in their corner. All except Rhea.

Mia slips her hands around Q's waist.

Q grins, cheeks flushed, as Mia leans in and kisses her. Q kisses her back.

And then, out of nowhere, Rhea dashes right past me.

An election of great success!

From your new president, Roger Vallance

While waiting for the official election figures, one thing has become clear. We, the Dutch people, have overwhelmingly chosen real change. With an estimated 30 to 33 seats in the House of Representatives, the Party for the People has won by a landslide!

Your message is loud and clear! We are through with old politics. It is time for renewal. Let us come together, and put our country first, once and for all.

You can rest assured that we will not break our election promises. From day one, every member of the PFTP will be committed to making good on our promises—to give everyone what they are entitled to. To make the Netherlands powerful again!

Starting tomorrow, we'll get to work at full speed. Tomorrow we begin forming a strong coalition in which your rights and needs come first. From there, we continue on the path to a better Netherlands—and today is just the beginning. Today, we celebrate!

Starting tomorrow, we dedicate our work to you. Starting tomorrow, we begin forming a strong coalition in which your rights and needs come first. Starting tomorrow, we continue on the path to a better Netherlands—but today, we celebrate!

Together, we are stronger. PFTP!

For more information or to donate, click <u>here</u>!

6.7M likes
1.2M comments
62,873 shares

TWENTY-THREE
109,364

Rhea rams into Mia like a bulldozer. Both Mia and Q topple off the crate and tangle on the floor. Q ends up beneath Mia, and before they can readjust, Rhea grabs Mia's throat with a furious cry and slams her head against the concrete.

Nora's chilling scream echoes through the Hangar.

With a gasp, Mia looks around wild-eyed, clearly in shock.

My throat constricts. I have to do something, but my legs refuse to budge.

"Keep your paws off her!" Spit flies from Rhea's mouth as she yells at Mia. "Keep your filthy paws off her!"

She slams Mia's face against the concrete again. I hear a sickening *crack*, and a red pool grows around her head.

Q tries to crawl away, but her hands are still trapped behind her back, bound by Mia's sweater. Her mouth opens with a soundless scream.

Rhea's attention is locked on Mia, her eyes wide as she watches her bleed.

Finally, I snap out of my trance and fly off my mattress. My arm clutches Rhea's neck and works her to the ground. She doesn't even resist me. It's like she's letting this happen.

Frankie rushes to help me.

"No! No!" Rhea shouts, her voice breaking. "I didn't mean to..."

I keep my arm wrenched around Rhea's neck as Frankie grabs hold of her legs, keeping her still. I apply more pressure to her throat until all that comes out of her mouth is a gurgling, screeching noise. Tears well in her eyes until her whole body starts to shake.

Rhea goes limp.

I release her and dive over to Mia. Her face is pale, and the pool of blood around her head is even larger now. My heart beats in my throat as I brainstorm how to save her. She's losing too much blood.

Frantically, I untie the sweater from Q's wrists and press it against Mia's wound.

"Harder!" Frankie urges, but I'm already pushing as hard as I can. I try to think of another way to help, but deep down, I know it's over. She's still losing too much blood. It's on my hands, my cheeks, the floor. There's blood *everywhere*.

Q crawls over to Mia, sobbing. Nora is already beside her, holding Mia's limp hand.

I vaguely register the Long-Termers dragging Rhea's unconscious body away.

"What should I do?" Silent tears roll down my cheeks. "She keeps bleeding!"

So much blood. Everywhere I look.

I try to remember the first aid classes I took during citizenship training, but I'm blanking.

"I..." Mia's voice sounds groggy, and her eyes roll back in their sockets.

"Frankie!" My voice hitches fearfully as I cry out.

"Sin, I..." Frankie's voice falters, as if she refuses to utter the words we're all thinking. "I don't think there's anything we can do for her anymore."

Together, we sit by Mia as she closes her eyes, her breathing slowing down.

After thirteen drawn-out breaths, she stops. Her chest falls, without rising again, and for a moment, mine does the same. This can't be happening.

Her wristband begins to flash, faster and faster—until the screen goes black.

For a minute, or maybe an hour, we sit silently together, Q and Nora holding Mia's hands.

"Come on." Frankie's voice sounds empty.

With a heavy weight on my chest, I help her move Mia's body. Nora wipes the blood on her face away with a wet towel.

I stare at a girl who was beginning to feel more and more like a friend. If I didn't know any better, I'd think she was sleeping.

Frankie's comforting arm finds a way around my shoulders, and her fingers caress my skin. "You did everything you could." Gently, she leads me to the shower room. "You should wash off."

I know she's right. My body is sticky with sweat and blood, but I feel no desire to shower. It's pointless. Mia's dead.

When I don't make an effort to undress myself, Frankie does it for me. She turns on the faucet and holds her hand under it. "The water's lukewarm, but I can't do any better," she whispers, stepping out of the cubicle. "I'll wait over here."

I step forward and let the water flow down my arms. I stare at the floor, where the water runs less and less red. Maybe Vallance is right. Maybe we're all animals in here, and it's a good thing we're killing each other off.

Or is it the Hangar that turns us into monsters?

Eventually, the water runs clear. It feels like, along with the color red, a piece of Mia has spilled down the drain too.

I couldn't save her. A loud sob rises from the depths of my stomach, and I can't help but collapse onto the tile.

I cry until my throat is raw and my cheeks are chapped. How am I supposed to survive in here for two more months?

A soft knock on the cubicle door snaps me out of my daze. "Sin?"

I want to say something, but my voice is gone.

Slowly, the door opens, and Frankie enters my cubicle. She turns off the water and wraps a towel around me. Only when I'm completely covered does she meet my gaze. In her eyes, I see my sadness reflected. This hurts more than I can bear. Her strong arms help me up, and without turning her eyes away, she rubs me dry. I lay my head on her shoulder, and she presses her lips to my forehead. The warmth of her breath makes my skin tingle.

Once she's done drying me, she offers my clothes and steps out of the cubicle.

I force myself to tug my jogging suit on, then let Frankie lead me back to our mattresses.

With my back to Mia's dead body, I lie down. Frankie cuddles up to me and puts her hands on my shoulders.

"Are you okay?" Her fingers caress my cheek.

"No," I answer. "I can't do this. I can't watch more girls beat each other up. I can't stay here any longer."

Frankie looks at me pensively, a fierceness in her eyes. "You mean it?"

"Yes. No." I sigh as I try to form a coherent thought. "I mean, yes, of course I want to leave. But the only way to get out of here early is to die."

Frankie begins to sit up. Supporting herself on her forearms, she looks straight into my eyes and whispers, "What if there's another way?"

TWENTY-FOUR
109,331

"Another way?" I don't understand what Frankie's driving at. "Either you stay here until your time is up, or you die. Those are the options."

"I'm serious." She grabs my hand and leads me back to the shower room. *What is she up to?*

Frankie tugs me into the last cubicle, puts her sock on the drain, and twists the nozzle. Water pools around the sock. She sighs, turns the water off, and sits on the floor. "I don't know if I'm doing the right thing by telling you this, but I can't just do nothing. Not after what you said. Not now that we're outnumbered, and hungry, and getting weaker."

"What are you talking about?"

"At the same time, I really don't want to risk your life." She grabs my shoulders and shakes her head. "You're too important to me. Your little brother is waiting for you. He needs you."

I shake her hands off. "Just get it out already."

"It's better to show you." She dips her finger into the water pooling around the drain and slides it across the tile. The water leaves darker lines where her finger draws a rectangle. "If this is the Hangar..."

She dips her finger in the water again and draws a smaller rectangle bordering one side of the larger one. "And this is where the switch cell is, and here we have the yard..." She draws a square next to yet another side of the Hangar.

"Okay?"

I watch her scatter dots around the building. "In the Hangar, they don't care what we're up to, but they don't want people trying to break us out either, so there are cameras outside. And here"—she draws a square outside the Hangar, diagonal from the switch cell, right behind our sleeping area —"is the power supply."

"How do you know all this?"

"I told you, my dad has the blueprints on his computer, and I have his password. That's how I know about a blind spot, an area the cameras can't monitor." She points to the space between the Hangar and the generator. "If we dig right here"—she draws a cross on the wall—"we can escape."

I stare at her drawing. The first lines she drew are already starting to fade, but my mind is blown. "But... How... Why didn't you say any of this before?"

"Believe me, I've been on the verge of telling you so many times. When I saw you digging outside. When Nora was attacked in the kitchen. When I showed you my drawings. But I didn't, because it's just... too risky. I can't claim with full certainty that the cameras weren't changed after I studied the blueprints, and once you take off your wristband, there's no turning back. Until now, it was safer to just do our time here, but now... things are different."

I bite my lip.

"I'm going to sit with Mia, okay? Think about it." Frankie presses a kiss to my temple and steps out of the cubicle.

Dazed, I lean against the wall and watch her lines fade. There's a way out of here. A way to be with Cross again. But if I take him and flee, what would happen to Dad? Could I bring him too? Would he *want* to come with us?

I grip my head. It feels like my brain's about to explode. How am I sup-posed to decide if this is worth the risk?

Especially when that risk could mean the end of everything...

Or the beginning.

It takes me a moment to remember how to move my legs again. I walk to Frankie with leaden steps. I know she wants an answer, but I can't give her one. Not yet.

Frankie is hunched over, holding Mia's hands, murmuring to herself.

I put my hand on her shoulder so as not to startle her.

"I need time."

Frankie looks over at me. "Take as much time as you need. We have to say goodbye to Mia first, anyway. Hopefully the new supplies will arrive tomorrow, so we can put her body in the switch cell. In the meantime, get some rest."

I don't protest. I lie on my mattress and pull the blanket up as far as I can. I fear that I'll have to fight my whirring thoughts all night—but my body is far too spent, and soon, I drift away.

A gentle hand shakes me awake, and when I open my eyes, I stare right into Frankie's. "I let you sleep as long as I could, but it's time."

Reality hits me—we're about to say goodbye to Mia. With a dry mouth, I sit up straight and rub the tension out of the muscles in my neck. The others are already lined up around Mia's bed.

I join them and stand next to Q. She pats my shoulder briefly, not averting her gaze from the bedsheet that covers Mia's body.

"Today, we're saying farewell to someone who was very dear to all of us." Frankie's voice trembles, and I watch her roll her shoulders back in an attempt to stay upright. "Someone we will carry in our hearts for the rest of our lives. Someone who made our time here at the Hangar a little brighter, who made us laugh, who colored the gray days. Someone gone too soon, who had a whole life ahead of her. Someone who didn't deserve to die."

The first person to step forward and pay her respects is Nora. With trembling fingers, she places a folded crane on top of the bedsheet. And another, and another, until Mia is surrounded by seventeen paper birds. "I hope you'll fly with the birds, Mia. Forever free."

Nora walks back and puts her head on Q's shoulder. Q caresses her for a moment before stepping forward herself. "You were a good person. You made the Hangar a little better. I'm going to miss you."

Frankie and I step forward last. I put my palm on what I think is Mia's hand under the sheet. "I'm sorry. If only I could have done more for you."

Frankie tightens her grip on my shoulder. "People say you can't make friends in the Hangar. That everyone's too cruel in here. But you're proof that they're wrong about us. I'll never forget you."

The ominous scraping of the switch cell drowns out her last words.

"It's time."

We grab the end of the sheet we wrapped Mia in, and together, carry her to the cell.

Three of the five Long-Termers are already there. No Rhea. No Milou. Without saying a word, they take the new supplies out of the switch cell— even the two crates of new phones, an extra to make up for our missed delivery. I sigh in relief when I notice them carrying the food straight to the kitchen.

I help the others lay Mia on the cold, steel floor of the switch cell. Then I gently place our crate of disassembled phones next to her.

I look at Mia one last time before the switch cell door closes in front of us.

She almost made it out alive.

TWENTY-FIVE
108,852

I don't sleep a wink that night. The AC comes on an hour after we turn the phones in. And although I'm grateful for the cool air, the rumbling suddenly feels intrusive.

Instead of falling asleep, I stare into the darkness and think. About the risks. About the odds of getting caught. About the chance we won't survive. About the fact that more of my friends might die. But also about the possibility that it'll work out. That I could be free. *Truly* free.

When the lights come on and the others wake up, I've made my decision. Frankie's plan is all we have. This is my only chance to help Cross.

I find Frankie in the kitchen, sitting on the floor, watching Nora make sandwiches.

I lower myself next to Frankie and lay my head on her shoulder, so my lips are close to her ear.

"I think we should do it," I whisper.

"Me too."

"What about the others?"

Frankie faces me. "We should at least tell Nora and Q."

I follow Frankie back to the mattresses, and she calls Nora and Q for a gathering. She tells them everything she knows, in one steady stream of words, and once she's done, everything is quiet. We sit and wait for their delayed reactions.

Finally, Q's face fills with anger. "Why didn't you tell me? You knew I wanted to escape!"

"Because it's a crazy plan." Nora glares at Q. "We'll never get through that wall. And if by some miracle we manage, we'll be shot as soon as we set one foot outside the Hangar."

"I'm sorry." Frankie grabs Q's hand. "I didn't dare tell you. It's a big risk, much bigger than you realize."

Q's eyes sharpen. "And my situation is far more hopeless than you realize."

Frankie sighs. "You're right. Look, I can't guarantee anything, but the wall isn't nearly as sturdy as it looks." She pulls a toothbrush out of her pocket, the back of which she's turned into a shiv. "It *will* be hard work though."

Her drawings, I realize. That's how she discovered that our walls aren't scrape-proof.

"Sin and I are going to try," Frankie continues. "I can't make the choice for you, but if you want to come with us, you're welcome to."

"And the Long-Termers?" Nora shoots a hesitant glance over her shoulder at their sleeping area.

"No way," I interject, finally joining their conversation. I know I'm being harsh and callous, but we can't run any more risks. "They've made their choice. I won't let them ruin my one chance for freedom."

"In that case, we have to make sure they don't find out," Nora says.

"The Long-Termers have no reason to enter our sleeping area," I reply. "We can prop up Mia's mattress, and use it to shield the hole as we work."

Q crosses her arms, a determined look settling around her lips. "Just point out where I should start."

Frankie gestures to where our sleeping area runs into the shower room wall, and I drop onto her bed. My head is pounding, and I want nothing but complete silence for a while. I close my eyes and try to shut out the sounds of the Hangar, but pretty soon, I hear the scraping of Q's sharpened toothbrush against the wall.

I cover my ears with my hands and wait for sleep to take me.

***

Nora's tense voice rouses me from sleep. "I'm coming with you. Nothing you say can stop me." She stands behind Q, scowling, her arms crossed.

"No you're not!" snaps Q, turning to face her. For a moment, I fear she'll lunge at Nora, but then her voice softens. "You have a future. Once you get out of here, you'll be old enough to emancipate yourself, become a legal adult. Then you can get your high school diploma and apply for art school. You can't give all that up." She's practically pleading now.

"But I want to stay with you." Nora stubbornly juts out her chin. "You know as well as I do that they won't give a Hangar child any emancipation rights, especially with all the files out there about the mess I caused in the Children's Facility. I don't fit in their system."

Q sighs. "You don't realize how dangerous this is."

"I'm not a toddler. I understand more than you think." Nora's face reddens. "I don't want to go back into the system." Her wrist jerks, and her face contorts from pain.

Q covers her face with both hands and takes a deep breath. A moment passes before she drops her fists to her sides, tense and trembling. Her expression is hard, but there's sorrow in her eyes. "Then understand this: I don't *want* to take you with me. I don't want some child holding me back. You'll only be a burden."

Her words hit me like a whip, and I look from Q to Nora, my eyes widening. Tears run down Nora's cheeks, her face contorting.

I see Q swallow before she turns her head away. She doesn't even meet Nora's gaze.

Nora's mouth opens as if she wants to say something, but she closes it again and runs for the showers.

"That was harsh." Frankie glances at the crying girl.

"I had to do *something*." Q looks desperate. "I can't let her throw her future away."

"And what do you think that future will look like in here?" Frankie's voice is flat. "Nora, surviving with the likes of Rhea and Milou as her only company?"

With a curse, Q throws the toothbrush down and storms after Nora.

Frankie looks back at me. "If we work in shifts and keep scraping at this rate, we could be out of here in a week."

"And what else do we do until then?" A week feels short enough to touch the end of my time here, yet far enough that Q might as well have said we're waiting on a presidential pardon.

"We have to decide who's coming with us. And we need to pack supplies —food and water. Maybe we can turn our spare sweaters into some kind of sling, though we likely won't be able to bring enough supplies for more than a few days." Frankie's face is serious. "After that, we'll have to find a new source of food—and normal clothes, because we'll stand out too much in these jumpsuits."

"What about our wristbands?"

"I thought it might be smart not to take them off simultaneously. We can't risk the Guard getting suspicious, and coming here to take a look."

I nod. It's a good plan, but who's going to be first? I sigh and focus on Frankie's face. She has dark bags under her eyes.

"I'll take care of the next few hours of work." I pick up a toothbrush and get down on my knees in front of the hole. "You go get some sleep. Once we're outside, you never know when you'll be able to spend the night on a real mattress again."

Frankie slides her hand down my back. "Just a little longer, and we'll be free together."

I smile and get to work.

It doesn't take long for my whole right arm to hurt. I use my left hand instead, but that doesn't go nearly as fast, so I keep working with my right hand anyway, despite the pain. There's a small pile of debris next to me— the girls who worked on the wall earlier swept it into the corner as best they could.

I try to imagine what my life will be like once we actually get through this wall. I may be on the run, but I'll be able to live life on my own terms. Together with Cross. Or should I still try to convince Dad to come with us, even with all the risks involved?

I sit up. The uneven, hard floor cuts into my knees, and the cold seeps through my shins, deep into my bones.

Being alone with my own thoughts is exhausting—discussions always end up being pointless. There's always a counter-argument waiting, so I think in circles until I want nothing more than to turn my brain off for a few minutes.

Nora and Frankie handle their thoughts better than I do. Nora has her origami and Frankie has her drawings, but I'm not creative. I have no hidden talents, nothing to get me out of my own head, and those stupid phones don't help at all.

I switch arms again, bending and stretching the fingers of my cramped hand one by one.

Soft footsteps resound behind me. Maybe Frankie's feeling restless?

The moment I turn around, a strong arm wraps itself around my throat.

FROM OUR ARCHIVES:
Bill passed to revise correctional facilities

From your president, Roger Vallance

Early this morning, the proverbial die was cast. Our plan to reform the prison system was passed in the Senate by a majority vote.

We hereby list the main points of this proposal for your convenience:

- Budgets for juvenile detention centers will be cut by 20%. All focus within these institutions will be on re-educating young offenders. There will be more time for reflection and rehabilitation. Practices such as drug trafficking and extortion within juvenile facilities will be punished more severely.

- Budgets for adult correctional facilities will be cut by 50%. Close to a quarter of prisons will close this year, and within those that remain open, recreation rooms will be converted into extra cells.

- As of January 1st of next year, all psychiatric clinics will be permanently closed. A reoffending rate approaching 30% is too high to justify the enormous costs.

- Effective immediately, there will be a hiring freeze in the Justice Department. Our goal is a 25% workforce reduction by the end of the year. As inmates will be spending more time in their cells, we can afford to reduce staff. All Justice Department employees will be offered a retraining course to prepare them for jobs in healthcare or law enforcement.

These efforts will help us save over 5 million guilders annually—money that will directly benefit your healthcare, your education, and your safety!

Together, we are stronger. PFTP!

For more information or to donate, click <u>here</u>!

7.2M likes
1.9M comments
74,863 shares

TWENTY-SIX
108,830

I gasp for breath, but my throat is squeezed shut. Even when I thrash around wildly, my kicks only meet empty air.

Someone lifts me by the neck, and black spots dance before my eyes. I kick backward as hard as I can. My heel grazes something.

Again, I try to suck air into my lungs, but I only manage to make a soft wheezing sound.

"Tell me! Tell me what you plan to do with them."

I can't reply. The black spots are getting bigger, darker, and double by the second, blocking my vision.

Suddenly, I see Cross flash in front of my eyes, pushing through the blur.

I can't give up.

Once more, I kick back, this time a little more to the left.

My heel stings from the hit, and my attacker groans in my ear. Her arm around my throat slackens slightly. Rasping, I let air rush into my lungs as I flail my arms about, hoping to break free.

Something soft and damp meets my right hand. Instantly, I know something's wrong.

The toothbrush has sunk into her upper arm. I let go in sheer terror. With a pained face, Rhea grabs hold of the toothbrush and pulls it out of her, a red stain blooming on her sleeve.

Without thinking, I take off my sweater and press it against the wound.

"Forget it." Rhea brushes my hand away. With her good arm, she gestures to the hole in the wall. "Just tell me what *this* is."

"I think it's pretty obvious. You're not stupid, right?"

"But *you* are, if you seriously think it'll work."

I sigh. "Why are you here, Rhea?"

"I wanted to make sure you weren't plotting revenge." Her voice falters. "I *have* to protect the other Long-Termers." She seems so convinced, so cockily sure that she's the only one who can help them.

"I didn't mean to..." The words stick in the back of my throat as I stare at her bleeding arm. "You scared me."

"I didn't mean to either. Killing Mia, I mean." Her shoulders droop, and her eyes are blank. I've never seen Rhea look defeated like this before. "I just wanted her to let go of Q. And Q didn't even have a chance to say no. *Everyone* should have a chance to say no." She turns her head away and swallows hard.

"But... it was just a silly lapdance. A joke. Q *liked* it."

Rhea shrugs and looks past me, at the hole. "You know this isn't going to work, right?"

I keep quiet.

"But I guess everyone needs *something* to believe in," Rhea continues. "I won't tell the others." She nods before leaving our part of the Hangar.

My gaze trails from the hole in the wall to the bloody toothbrush on the floor. I grab it and feel the warm, sticky blood between my fingers.

I begin to scrape again.

So much violence. So much blood. It's all too much.

Outside, everyone thinks the Hangar is this great success story. In one interview, Vallance called it both a punishment and a blessing—an opportunity for penance and the chance to start fresh with a clean slate. Research, *his* research, showed that complete isolation from the wrong environment causes young people to start thinking about how to turn their lives around.

By now, I know better, even though I've only served a small fraction of my 100 days. The Hangar didn't teach me anything that wasn't already inside of me. I can make friends. I can love. I can fight for what I believe in.

And fundamentally, I know I'm not a bad person. I'm not a saint, nor an angel, but I always follow my heart.

I keep scraping, on and on.

"Good morning." Nora's cheerful voice shakes me out of my thoughts. Apparently I've been working all night. "I brought you a sandwich."

"Thank you." I gratefully accept the food and take a big bite.

"I could do this for a while. So you can just eat."

"Gladly." I hand her the toothbrush.

"It's okay. Q made an extra." Her gaze drifts to the dried blood on the handle and hairs, but she doesn't bring it up.

I tuck the shiv into the elastic of my pants, swallow the last bite of my sandwich, and head for the shower room to wash my hands. I roll up my sleeves and let the cold water run over my skin.

My gaze lands on my wristband.

108,812

It's time to get moving. I can't stay here for much longer, living with this seemingly endless countdown. I also can't return to a system that will put me under surveillance for the rest of my life, in which I, and the people I love, will never be truly free.

I remove the toothbrush from my pants and hook the sharp end under the strap of my wristband. With a deep breath, I snap it in two.

Silently, I look at the blinking screen.

A moment later, it turns black.

It's over. And I'm okay with that.

Frankie lies on her mattress with her eyes closed. With a smile, I walk over and lift the blanket, curling up to her so we're spooning. I wrap my arm around her body and pull her even closer. She shuffles sleepily, turning her head toward me, and I press a kiss to her lips. She smirks, rolls to fully face me, and gazes deeply into my eyes.

For a moment, I let go of everything—all that I've seen and all my doubts about tomorrow. For just a moment, her face, her warm eyes, and her friendly smile are all I see.

Her hand touches my freed wrist. "You took it off."

I nod. "Now we can really be together."

Her voice is soft. "Is this what love feels like?"

A warmth spreads through me, and I can't hold back my grin. "Yeah. Yeah, I think so."

TWENTY-SEVEN

I scrape and scrape and scrape—until suddenly, a ray of evening light peeks through. My heart hammers in my throat, and it feels like a hundred butterflies are fluttering in my stomach. We're almost free.

I turn to see Frankie leaning against the wall, her eyes closed in exhaustion.

"Look," I whisper, a little too loudly.

Frankie opens her eyes, turns my way, and flings her arms around my neck in pure elation. She kisses me. "We did it."

From that moment on, there's a palpable tension in our part of the Hangar. It reminds me of my first day of high school, when I stepped into a whole new world. I didn't know what the rules were, and I didn't know anyone. I felt totally, utterly lost.

The four of us get ready to leave. We stock up on food, take apart the entire week's quota of phones, and wash our clothes one last time.

The Long-Termers haven't been snooping around our sleeping area anymore. Maybe Rhea didn't tell them what she saw. Or maybe they know everything, and are curious to see what happens to us.

We continue scraping at the wall, expanding the little hole of light. I feel like it takes forever to make it big enough to crawl through. But eventually, the time comes, and with pounding hearts, we gather at our exit.

"I love you guys." Q looks at us one by one. "Whatever happens, we stick together."

The first to crawl out is Frankie. Her arm reaches back into the Hangar to receive our sweaters stuffed with supplies. Then she helps me out next. The wall is at least two feet thick, and the hole is barely large enough to squeeze through. The jagged bricks scrape my skin, but before I know it, I'm standing outside in the black of night.

Outside at last.

I squint in the darkness and make out an unkempt field that surrounds the Hangar. I think I see trees in the distance too—shelter from the security cameras. We just have to get there safely.

As Frankie helps Nora and Q, I finally look up—and the sight takes my breath away. Stars. For the first time in nearly a month, *constellations.*

A gentle breeze caresses my cheeks. No matter what happens, the Guard can't take this away from me. I focus on the North Star and think of Cross. I imagine him looking out the window right now, staring at the same sky. For the first time since I entered the Hangar, we are living in the same world.

"We have to go." Frankie's fingers close around mine, and my heart skips a beat—partly from her warmth, partly from the thrill of what comes next. Once we start walking, any step could be our last.

I look back one final time. Whatever happens, I vow to never set eyes on the Hangar again.

I refuse to be wallbound.

Frankie leads. She knows best where the cameras are—and in single file, Q, Nora, and I follow. We wade through the open field of tall, dead grass. Frankie's steps are even and determined, but her shoulders are tense. I can tell she's nervous, scared of accidentally stepping into a camera's view. Our lives are in her hands.

A *snap.*

We freeze.

My breathing speeds up, and my other hand clings to my bare wrist. Then I remember that my wristband is gone. My stress levels can no longer shock me.

Slowly, Frankie lifts her foot. "Twig," she whispers.

We sigh in relief, and start walking again. I don't risk looking at anything besides Frankie's back right in front of me. We cross the last stretch of the field, reaching the dark edge of the forest. It's eerily quiet. Even the birds seem to be holding their breath.

Stress falls from my shoulders when we step under the dense trees. They shield us from the moonlight, leaving us in total darkness. The cameras couldn't possibly see us now.

"Okay, what next?" Q's voice is close, and as my eyes adjust to the deeper darkness, I begin to make out her silhouette.

Everyone automatically turns to Frankie.

"We need to keep moving to increase the distance between us and the Hangar. I doubt they'll find out that we escaped, but we can never be too careful." Frankie treads deeper into the forest, and the three of us follow her quietly.

We cross through the trees, then through another field, and then more trees and fields. We don't stop until the first glow of morning sunlight tickles the horizon.

"We should find shelter and sleep for a few hours. Then we can look for new clothes. We stand out too much in these jumpsuits." Frankie points to a dilapidated barn farther down the meadow. "Let's rest in there."

When we step into the barn, the smell is the first thing I notice—a musty amalgamation of feces and hay. The floor's wooden planks have partly rotted away, creating wide gaps in several places. Iron fences divide the space into smaller cubicles, each less than a square yard. This must have been an old pigsty.

Q lingers at the doorway, her nose crinkled. "This is worse than the Hangar."

"But we can leave whenever we want." Nora giggles. "We don't have to stay here. And we can also lie outside, in the sun!"

"No," Frankie says firmly, scaring the smile off Nora's face. "We'd be too visible in the sun. This area may look deserted, but it's just a meadow out there—if anyone shows up, they'd see us instantly. We'll just have to deal with the smell."

We find the cleanest spot in the barn—in the corner, not far from the door—and open our makeshift backpacks. For some reason, our cold meals taste better now than they did in the Hangar.

Frankie offers to keep first watch, and I curl up against a hay bale, hoping to find a position comfortable enough to fall asleep in.

Next to us, Nora huddles up against Q, who strokes Nora's hair and begins to sing softly.

Somewhere very far from here
Is a place just for you
Where peace and freedom await
Come to that place, please do

Somewhere not so far away
A place full of love and joy
Where you can always be yourself
You'll never have to be coy

Secretly it's quite close by
With friends by your side
Where everyone loves you a lot
Where you don't have to hide

A place you carry with you
Without sorrow and pain
It's never far away from you
It's inside your heart, it will always remain

As the last note of Q's verse trails off, I close my eyes. I'd love to live in a place like the one she sang about in her song. With Cross by my side— and hopefully Frankie too.

Back in the Hangar, Q told me that most of her people managed to get away. Somewhere out there, they've established a new hideout. I just need to find it.

Yes, that's it. That's exactly what I'm going to do.

I'll return home with Frankie and explain everything to Cross. We'll take as much food and supplies as we can, and then we'll look for Q's people.

With a smile, I allow sleep to carry me away.

"Sin?"

Groaning, I open my eyes and look straight into Nora's face.

"Everyone's awake. It's time to go."

I hoist myself upright and walk to the other side of the barn to pee behind a wall.

When I return, Frankie offers me water. I drink the entire bottle in one go and put the empty container in my bag.

"What's the plan?" I ask her.

"There should be a main road nearby. Once we find a store, we can send Nora in, wearing just her bra and underwear. She'll tell the clerk that someone stole her clothes while she was swimming."

"Nice. Who wouldn't feel bad for an embarrassed young girl in her underwear?" Q says. "Plus, out of all of us, Nora looks the most innocent. We can assume the clerk will walk to the back of the store to call for help, and then Nora can quickly grab some clothes for us and run out."

"I'll come with her," I say. "Why would anyone go swimming alone? If we show up together, as sisters, it'd be more believable—and we could grab even more clothes on our way out."

Frankie looks like she's about to object, but before she can, Q nods. "Good idea!"

Together, we trudge through the meadow. Even though the sun's already setting, the summer heat is still oppressive at this hour. Sweat runs down my back in multiple trails. These Hangar jumpsuits are completely unsuitable for outdoor hiking.

Relief washes over me when we finally reach the main road Frankie mentioned—a sign of civilization at last. We follow the road until we reach a block of stores. Through the window, we see that one of them sells clothes, so we hide behind the building, out of sight from passersby.

Nora and I take off our jumpsuits. Frankie and Q also take off their sweaters, preparing to slip on the stolen clothes as soon as we return with them.

It's hard not to stare at Frankie. Scars peek out from under her bra, stretching from her back to her shoulders. They are dark, but beautiful.

She is beautiful.

"Let's go." Nora sounds determined. She hugs Q and drags me to the store.

A soft bell jingles as we push the door open. The air conditioner is on full blast, and goosebumps spring across my arms immediately.

"Good afternoon, can I help..." A man with a beer belly and a mustache pops up from behind the counter. "Oh, my goodness! What happened to you girls?"

Nora conjures an innocent face. "We were swimming, my sister and I, and then some bratty boys thought it'd be funny to steal our clothes."

"Were they three guys with long hair, by any chance?"

She nods.

"Those rotten eggs always come to my store to mess around too. Even the Hangar couldn't help guys like them. Could I call someone for you?"

"Please." Nora rattles off a fake phone number, and I have to stop myself from looking at her in surprise. She's a mighty good actor.

"You girls wait here." The man disappears to the back of the store.

My heart beats wildly as we tear new clothes off the racks. I grab an armful of T-shirts and snatch a bunch of cardigans. How long has that guy been gone? In all this hurrying, I feel lost without my wristband, with no way to keep track of time. Nervous jitters churn in my stomach, but I shove them aside and grab more stuff.

"We have to go now," I whisper in a trembling voice.

Nora nods. We step out the door, and that damn bell jingles again.

"What..." The man runs after us, cellphone in hand. "Hey!"

We round the building's corner as fast as we can.

"Guys, run!" My voice hitches. "Get out of here!"

TWENTY-EIGHT

With our arms full of clothes, Nora and I race down the road, leading the way.

"Keep going!" I yell.

Nora drops a few items, and I stumble to grab them in her trail. My heart beats in my throat and when I risk looking back. Behind Frankie and Q, the furious clerk is still after us, holding his cellphone to his ear.

He's calling the Guard!

It's only a matter of time before the Guard gets us. What if they send drones? The question echoes in my mind, like a needle stuck in the groove of an old record. Meanwhile, my legs keep moving. I run faster than ever before, but my stamina's fading. I'm losing my breath. I barely manage to catch up with Nora. Q and Frankie are right behind me.

Once more, I glance over my shoulder. I'm grateful that the clerk isn't in the best shape, but the anger on his face is evident, even from a distance.

Q, Frankie, and I manage to keep going, but Nora loses her lead and falls behind us.

The man is closing in fast.

Without giving it a second thought, I double back and run straight at Nora.

I'm too late, though. She screams when the man grabs her arm and slings her to the pavement. I leap onto him, my fist striking just below his ribs, and he sinks to the ground, groaning. He won't be down for long. I quickly help Nora upright and drag her over to Frankie and Q.

The man calls after us as he pushes himself up, using swear words my dad would gasp at.

We keep moving, and just as I think the man's about to keep running, a stone hits him smack in the head. I'm not sure which of the other three girls threw it, but it doesn't really matter.

The man groans and rubs his head. Blood trickles between his fingers.

I don't have time to feel sorry for him. We *have* to get out of here.

We keep running for about ten minutes before sirens begin to wail in the distance. I look around in desperation. We're in the middle of the suburbs. All around us are spacious houses with large gardens. There's not a hedge or alley in sight that we could hide in.

The sirens are approaching, and now I also hear the distinctive hum of drones in the air. My heart beats even faster. I can't stop panting. I'm afraid I might pass out.

"There!" Frankie points to a house in the distance. The curtains are closed and there's a *FOR SALE* sign in the yard. Its grass is overgrown—no one has lived there for a while.

Alarm bells ring in my head. Houses are never just left empty—not for long, anyway. But the literal alarm bells of the sirens weigh heavier.

We dart into the yard and crouch behind the fence separating it from the neighbor's. Frankie scans the area, then strides to the door and slams her foot against it with a grunt. With a loud *crack*, her lower leg disappears halfway through. She yanks it back, reaches through the hole, and unlocks the door from the inside. "After you, girls!"

Nora runs in first, and once all four of us are inside, Frankie closes the door. She tries to camouflage the hole as best she can by jamming the loose pieces of wood back in. We can only hope the Guard won't look too closely.

There's a closet in the hallway. We hide inside and huddle up together in the darkness.

Now we wait.

Nora's still gasping for air, and Q hums at her reassuringly.

Frankie grabs my hand and squeezes it gently. The sirens slowly fade into the distance.

The house is quiet. I let out a deep breath. *That was a close call.*

"Wow!" Nora holds up a flashlight she found in here, using it to illuminate the closet shelves. They all hold the same thing—rows and rows of canned tomato soup. "The person who lived here sure liked soup a lot."

We leave the closet to explore the house, each of us carrying a few soup cans. Once we gather in the kitchen, Q opens a drawer and holds up a can opener. "At least we'll have some food tonight." Then she cocks an eyebrow. "Besides the can opener, there's only knives in here—and they're no butter knives, if you know what I'm saying."

Frankie runs to the drawer and pulls out a full-blown *machete*. "I'm sure this will come in handy."

I study the bookshelves in the living room—they're also stocked with canned soup. The few books I manage to find have titles that Vallance surely wouldn't approve of: *What To Do When the World Ends, Survival After the Apocalypse, Ten Essential Survival Skills.*

I'm convinced the person who lived here didn't leave voluntarily, considering how their weapons remain. Maybe the Guard sent them to the Drain or one of the Houses of Mental Retention: the place for people who've lost their grip on reality.

For a long time, I was afraid they'd send Dad to one of those, especially after Mom left. Sometimes he left the house to go to work, but sometimes he couldn't manage that. He'd sit in front of the TV, swearing and ranting at the news.

"We can eat the tomato soup cold," Nora says. "I just can't find any bowls, so everyone can have their own can." She starts opening cans while everyone else changes into new clothes.

"Are you okay?" I give Nora a searching look. "Did the store attendant hurt you?"

Nora grimaces. "Not as much as you hurt him. Nice slap!"

"I'm serious."

She shrugs. "So am I. We got away. I'm fine."

"If you say so."

"Then we believe you," Q butts in. "I'm gonna check upstairs." She gets up and leaves the room.

"Dinner's ready!" Nora sounds so cheerful, and for a moment, it feels like nothing awful has happened. Like we're just a bunch of friends having dinner together.

I never had any friends before this.

Nora arranges the cans in a circle on the floor and sits down behind one. She wraps her hands around the can, puts it to her lips and takes a big sip.

"If you imagine that it's hot, it's actually quite nice."

The ceiling creaks above us—Q is still walking around upstairs. Everyone hesitantly starts on their soup.

Nora made it sound too good. The cold soup is way too thick, and the bits of tomato are grainy and stick to my palate.

From Frankie's face, I can tell she's also struggling to stomach this.

"Look what I found!" Q joins us downstairs with the biggest first aid kit I've ever seen. "I'm sure it'll come in handy." She plops the duffel bag down, sits beside Frankie, and grabs a can of soup.

Then we all freeze. The sirens roar back to life, louder than ever, and colored lights slice through the cracks in the curtains.

They found us.

FROM OUR ARCHIVES:
Crime down 34% in three years

From your president, Roger Vallance

Large-scale research by the CBS has confirmed what you, as a citizen, have long known: in the past three years, crime in the Netherlands has shrunk by more than a third. The combination of universal basic income, a stronger police force, and tougher penalties have achieved what was almost unimaginable in previous years. This drastic decline in theft, robbery, assault, and other crimes proves that our theories are correct.

The task now is to bring these numbers down even further, and that can be done in two ways:

1. **Increased border patrol:** The same study from CBS shows that over 75% percent of thefts are committed by people who were not born in this country. Our first step to changing this is to speed up the procedure to leave the European Union.

2. **Accepting that not everyone can be saved:** Some people commit crimes solely because they enjoy seeing others suffer. For these individuals, no sentence is too harsh. From now on, they will be placed outside the normal prison population. Further plans are in development.

We are proud of these numbers, but we do not intend to stop here.

This is just the beginning.

Together. Stronger. PFTP!

For more information or to donate, click here!

8.1M likes
87,336 shares

TWENTY-NINE

"We have to get out of here." Frankie's tone is dry and matter-of-fact. She stuffs the machete into the first aid duffel bag, slings its strap over her shoulder, and hurries through the back door.

We follow her into the backyard. The grass comes up to my knees, and the bushes are nothing like the perfectly trimmed hedges in the other yards I saw earlier. There's a fence surrounding the yard's perimeter with a single exit gate—Q and Nora have already stepped through it.

I stare at the open gate and realize that escaping as a group of four isn't practical. We should split up—Frankie and I could branch off alone.

I'm rooted to the ground. Frankie notices my hesitation and leans in, her hand sliding to the back of my neck to pull me closer. For a moment I think she's about to kiss me, but instead, she turns her head to whisper in my ear. "It's gonna be alright, Sin." Then she presses a kiss to my cheek and guides me to the gate.

Nora and Q are waiting just beyond the gate. They gesture for us to hurry.

We stand out less in civilian clothes, and the more distance we gain on the house—and with it, the sirens—the more my fear fades. But still, I keep feeling as though the Guard is right behind us. I can't avoid looking over my shoulder at every sound of rustling leaves or crackling branches. But there is nothing to see.

When evening falls, my muscles are aching. I regret not drinking all of that gunky tomato soup. My stomach is grumbling and I want nothing more than to lie down on the floor and sleep.

I suppress a yawn and immediately feel Frankie's gaze on me.

"We need to find a place to sleep," she says.

I'm sure that'll be difficult. We're still in the suburbs, and there are few places sheltered enough to sleep in safety.

We walk on for a while longer and eventually reach a park, where a few people are out for their evening walks. The trees around the children's playground should provide some cover, and the grass looks soft and inviting. For once, I'm glad for the hot summer—we don't have to worry about the cold.

Frankie once again offers to take the first watch, and the rest of us find a spot in the grass to lie down.

I don't want to admit it, but I miss the safety of Frankie's arm around me. I miss having a blanket, curling my toes beneath it like I used to so the monsters in the dark couldn't reach me. I want to feel protected, even if it's only an illusion.

Yet sleep soon wins out, drowning the thoughts in my head.

<hr>

When I jolt awake, morning sunlight is already hitting my face. Frankie is still keeping watch on the slide, clutching the machete. I hope some unsuspecting child won't come running into the playground.

I sit up to find Q leaning against a tree, while Nora swings nearby, rocking back and forth with a wide grin. Her shoplifted pants are too long and drag on the ground, but that doesn't seem to bother her.

How long has it been since she last played like this?

Suddenly, Frankie jumps up. Her eyes are wide, the machete held out in front of her. In a few strides, I scale the playground structure to join her.

"I think I saw something," she whispers. "Make sure Nora and Q are ready to run. I'll try to get a closer look."

I nod and run back to the swings. The huge smile on Nora's face contrasts my nagging sense of dread. I quickly pass on Frankie's message and stuff our supplies back into the jumpsuit bag. My stomach churns when I realize that we're running low on food. We'll have to get money from somewhere —or steal again, despite the risks.

A scream rises in the air, coming from Frankie's direction. I sprint towards her. When I round the corner, Frankie is leaning over someone.

Rhea?

"What are you doing here?" Frankie has Rhea's shirt clenched in her fist, and with her other hand, she presses the trembling machete against her throat. "Are you alone?"

"Yes, of course I'm alone! I ordered the others to stay put; they still have a shot at a normal life outside."

"Give me one good reason why I shouldn't slit your throat right here and now."

"I don't have one. Just do it."

The machete starts to shake more violently, and I put my hand on Frankie's shoulder. "She poses no threat. If you cut her throat in broad daylight, the Guard will never get off our case."

"We can't just let her walk, though." Frankie's jaw tenses, and she refuses to put the machete away. "What if she turns us in? Tells the Guard we're from the Hangar?"

"How stupid do you think I am? If I betray you, I betray myself too. I'll never let the Guard take me again. Not while I'm alive." Rhea cautiously tries to get up, but Frankie applies more pressure to the blade.

"Then why are you here?" I ask. Something in Rhea's gaze makes me doubt her words—makes me think there might be more behind this.

She shrugs. "I assumed you girls knew your way around. You weren't hard to track. Footprints, broken branches, discarded clothes. I erased most of your tracks. They won't be able to find you anymore. If you erase your own tracks from now on, that is."

Q stands protectively in front of Nora. "You don't expect us to say thank you, right?"

"I don't."

I give Frankie a look, and she pulls back the machete.

"Can you keep doing it?" I ask Rhea, helping her up.

"Keep doing what?"

"Covering our tracks. Making sure the Guard and the drones don't find us anymore."

Both Q and Frankie look at me with bewildered faces.

"You can't be serious!" Frankie exclaims. "She's not coming with us."

"Sin has a point." Nora rocks back and forth on the balls of her feet. "If we go on like this, it's only a matter of time before we get caught again. If Rhea can help us, it'd be stupid to refuse."

"As soon as you want to get rid of me, you can always cut my throat."

Rhea's comment throws Frankie off for a moment, but then she points the knife at her. "Fine. You can come. But I'm holding you to that offer."

THIRTY

Rhea proves useful—not just for covering our tracks, but also for general survival. She identifies edible plants, knows how to find clean drinking water, and helps us protect ourselves from the scorching sun.

When Nora asks Rhea how she knows so much, a dark expression crosses her face. Apparently she lived on the streets for a while. That's all she bothered to share.

As night falls, Rhea points us in the direction of a flower store. *CLOSED FOR THE SUMMER*, reads a sign on the door. Rhea uses a rock to smash a front window. She snakes her arm through the hole, and with a soft click, unlatches the door.

We go inside and find a place in the store to lie down. Luckily, there's a working restroom, which we take turns using. I drink clean water from the tap until my belly threatens to explode.

Rhea is the only one of us who doesn't immediately look for a place to rest. Instead, she rifles through the cupboards one by one. A few minutes later, she joins us with her arms full of old-fashioned chocolate bars.

"Wow!" Nora's eyes widen at the loot. "The people who work here must be good friends with the government."

"The owner's husband works as treasurer for the PFTP." Frankie points to a picture on the wall of a man handing a bouquet of flowers to President Vallance. "I've seen him at our house before."

I forgot that Frankie's father has some kind of high position in the government. I'm glad she doesn't have the same mindset as him. "Well, with money like theirs, I guess they won't miss the chocolate then," I say. "They could buy another stack, no problem."

Rhea gives each of us a bar and puts the rest next to Frankie. "Be smart and don't finish them all at once. I'm gonna check upstairs, see what's there."

Full of wonder, I look at the bar in my hand. It spells *Twix* in large letters. The golden packaging glistens in the light from the sign by the emergency exit. I open the wrapper carefully, trying to tear it as cleanly as possible, and take out the chocolate bar. I take a tiny bite and the taste explodes in my mouth. Cookie crumbs, chocolate, and caramel melt on my tongue. I can't suppress my sigh of utter delight. Next to me, Q has already finished her bar. Nora licks hers like it's a lollipop, and Frankie takes a single bite, only to put the rest aside.

The stairs creak as Rhea returns. Without looking at us, she puts down several bottles of drinks, a can of sausages, and a frozen loaf of bread. "There's a lot more food upstairs."

We eat our fill of half-frozen sausage sandwiches and, one by one, everyone falls asleep around me. I decide not to wake them and take the first watch, nibbling on the rest of my Twix.

"Can I sit next to you?" Rhea asks. I guess she's not asleep after all.

I shrug. It's not as if I can stop her, but I still don't completely trust her after what happened to Mia. I don't think I ever truly will. Yeah, it *seems* like she's trying to make amends, but she could also just be trying to save her own skin.

"Why did you follow us?"

Rhea sighs, but doesn't answer my question.

I hear Dad's voice in my head. *"Sin, you catch more flies with honey than with vinegar."*

I change tack. "I know you didn't mean to hurt Mia."

"And what if I did? She grabbed Q. She latched herself onto her body without permission, and you guys were cheering her on. You didn't even try to stop her."

My blood starts to boil. She's not making any sense. "Have you still not realized that you're in the wrong here? Q wasn't uncomfortable. She was having fun. I know that—"

"You don't know *anything*," Rhea cuts me off. Her body tenses up beside me.

"Because you're not *telling* me anything."

"What should I tell you? That I would never be a free woman had I stayed in the Hangar? That the Guard would only let me free if I served my time—*and* turned in the love of my life? That I've been doomed since birth?" With each word, the fire in her eyes extinguishes a little more. "All those girls in there? They're just stupid. They had good lives back home, but they ruined it for themselves."

I scoff and shake my head. She acts like she knows everything. Rhea has no clue who I am.

"Take Nora. She's an idiot. She ruined her only chance at a good life. Why attack the people who take care of you? I wish I'd been allowed to stay in the Children's Facility longer, but within six months of turning fourteen, you get kicked out. I *begged* them to stay. I offered to help out, to clean rooms... I would have done anything to stay, but they said it was time for me to become independent. All the people who took care of me there, who made me feel like I had a home for the first time in my life, dropped me like a bad habit, just because I aged out."

She sighs. "They sent me back home without hesitation. They said I could apply for emancipation and enter an assisted living program, but I already lost my trust in them. If the Children's Facility kicked me out, any assisted living program could do the same at the drop of a hat. The only way I could be absolutely sure I'd be safe was if I learned how to take care of myself. The first few weeks went pretty well. My mother seemed happy to have me home, and for a while, I was more important to her than her pills. She even sat with me sometimes, when I was doing homework." She bites her lower lip. "But the novelty of having me back wore off eventually. The call of the pills got stronger, and she relapsed."

Rhea's eyes turn glassy, and her voice gets tight. "Men started coming to the house more often again, and I wasn't allowed to leave my room while my mother took them to her bedroom. She became skinnier and skinnier. There were days I couldn't reach her at all. She'd just sit there on the couch, staring, not responding to anything I said or did. And when I couldn't take it anymore, I ran away. I thought I'd manage. I was almost fifteen—three more years and I would've been able to apply for my own house and a basic income. Three years seemed doable. I could eat free lunch at school, and in case of an emergency, I still had the key to my mother's house."

Rhea pauses, and I fill the silence without missing a beat: "It's never as easy as you think."

"No. It isn't. People claimed my mother was using our house as some kind of brothel, and once word spread that I was living on the streets too, no one wanted to be my friend anymore. During lunch break, the other kids made it a point to sit as far away from me as possible. And then, one day, some high school seniors followed me after school and ganged up on me in the park. They called me names. Talked bad about my mother. Said I must be like her. That I'd be up for it, surely." Rhea's face hardens, and a fiery spark flares in her eyes again. "I'll spare you the details."

My stomach contracts as the meaning of her words sink in.

She clamps her eyes shut. "In the end, Jay found me. He dealt with them and took care of me. From then on, it was us against the world. We did what was necessary to survive. The couples we robbed had more than enough, and we only targeted abusive men. We never hurt the women."

The story Q and Mia told me crosses my mind. They were closer to the truth than they themselves probably realized.

"When the Guard arrested me, they offered me the chance to betray Jay in exchange for a shorter sentence. But I would never betray him. *Never.* So they sent me to the Hangar.

"The last thing the high officer of the Guard said to me was, 'We assume you'll feel differently after a year in there—and if not, we can still send you to the Drain.'

"Just a few nights ago, I saw what you were doing with that hole, but I didn't tell the others. I waited until you disappeared, and then I took my chance." Rhea pauses. "It's my only chance to ever be free again."

THIRTY-ONE

I can't imagine how difficult the past few years must have been for Rhea, and yet one question keeps nagging me.

"You didn't answer my question," I declare. "Why did you come after us? There was a chance we might have killed you on the spot."

Rhea sighs. "Maybe part of me was hoping for that. An easy way out. I was planning to go off on my own, actually. Back to Amsterdam to see if I could find Jay—but then I saw your tracks. It was like a herd of elephants had been stomping through the woods. Might as well have put up a sign saying, *Escaped prisoners, this way!* I started erasing your tracks, and creating fake ones to throw the Guard off. It won't bring Mia back, but it's a way for me to make it up to you girls. I know you think I'm a bully, but I was just trying to protect everyone. No one should have to go through what I went through."

I'm not sure what to think. Could her good deeds ever make up for what happened to Mia?

Without making up my mind, I ask, "How about the others?"

"I left at night," Rhea explains. "I told Milou to keep them inside for now. Too many wristbands shutting down at once would be suspicious."

I let her words sink in.

"I'm not gonna stick around for long." Rhea seems to take my silence as disapproval. "I want to go back home, see how my mother's doing. I hope I can help her. Everyone deserves a second chance, or a third, or a fourth. As long as I stay indoors, no one will find out I'm with her."

"Do you really think people can change?"

She bites her lip. "I hope so. I hope *I* can change. I don't want to be afraid all the time, or feel like I have to draw blood to stay in control."

"I hope you'll manage."

"Tomorrow, after noon, I will go my own way. I advise you to do the same."

I give her a puzzled look.

"You realize that a group of four girls, all with buzz cuts, looks suspicious, right? Your chances will improve if you continue by yourself." She fidgets with her nails as she continues. "I assume you plan to stick with Frankie."

Her tone makes my guard go up. I take a slow breath, trying to keep my voice steady. "And?"

"I don't like the way she looks at you. Like you're a puzzle piece."

"Not *all* people are bad, Rhea." I let her words slide off me. "I hope someday you'll realize that."

"Maybe."

We sit silently together until Q comes to take the next watch. Without paying any more attention to Rhea's opinion, I curl up against Frankie and let sleep carry me away.

The sounds of plates and cups being put down shake me out of my nightmares. The busy noises remind me of life back at home, when Mom still lived with us and Dad would get up early on Sundays to fry eggs and bacon. I push myself up—I'm the last one awake.

The others are already sitting in a circle on the floor. In the center is a bowl filled with different kinds of sandwiches.

"Join us, Sin. Most of the sandwiches are thawed out now, and Rhea found a jar of chocolate spread somewhere." Nora beams at me. She's acting like the quarrel between her and Rhea never happened. Maybe she has a strong grasp of how important forgiveness is—or maybe she's just incredibly good at compartmentalizing. I can't tell.

Frankie moves aside, freeing up a spot next to her. She hands me a sandwich with a thick layer of chocolate spread in the middle. I lick along the edge, where a blob of chocolate oozes out between the two slices. I let it melt on my tongue, savoring the taste.

As we eat, Rhea says she's heading to Amsterdam. Anyone who wants to can travel with her, but the tone of her voice makes it clear she hopes no one will actually take her up on the offer.

I expect this to be the moment Frankie tells everyone that she and I will be moving on together as well, but she stays silent.

"Nora and I are headed for the southern border." Q puts her hand on her friend's knee. "I've heard great stories about Belgium. It seems to be a lot better there, at least for people like us."

Nora chuckles. "Q means *talented, intelligent young women with bright futures ahead of them!*"

I can't help but laugh, even though it stings a little. Mia would have made a joke like that.

"There's probably room for slightly less talented young women too." Q winks at Frankie and me. "I was hoping you might want to come with us."

I raise my palm. "No, I think we—"

"We need to travel together for a while, to get Sin's brother, and maybe her dad." Frankie doesn't look at me. "Seems smarter to take the coastal path to Rotterdam—the dunes always make a good hiding place. No one expects escaped convicts there. Plus, we can take baths in the ocean every night. Maybe we'll head your way after."

Q gives her a satisfied nod, stuffing the remainder of her sandwich into her mouth at once.

Meanwhile, I try to picture a map of the Netherlands in my head. I regret not paying more attention in geography class. If I'm imagining it right, we're still quite a ways from the coast—at least a few hours' walk to the west—while my hometown of Rotterdam lies almost directly south of here. Rhea's words about puzzle pieces run through my mind, but I push them away again. Frankie knows what she's talking about. If a detour is safer, it's the right choice.

FROM OUR ARCHIVES:
Festive opening of social workshops for convicts

From your president Roger Vallance

It all began with a dream—a vision of crime and punishment that no one had ever dared to develop before. How wonderful would it be if criminals were no longer sitting idly in prison cells, but instead repaying their debts to society through honest work?

Many plans did not pass the drawing board. After all, a good facility would need to satisfy several parties, which, at times, did not even seem possible. Considerations had to be made for the number of criminals, work across different education levels, and contributing to a better Netherlands—all without infringing on human rights.

Eventually, we came up with an institute that will be festively opened this weekend: a beautiful and modern drilling rig two hundred kilometers northwest of Texel. This platform contains thousands of solar panels, wind turbines, hydraulic turbines, and the manpower needed to keep them working. It will generate over 60% of our energy needs in an environmentally friendly way. Two birds with one stone: a cleaner and safer country for all.

8.4M likes
93,221 shares

THIRTY-TWO

The sun burns brightly as we walk along the river. It must be the weekend because the walkway is crowded by hikers, families with dogs and children, elderly couples holding hands, and bikers cycling at breakneck speed. No one gives us a second glance. With our stolen clothes, and hats and scarves that hide our short haircuts, it's like we belong here. Just four friends looking for a place to hang out.

The glint of sunlight on the water reminds me of when I was little, before my father had his accident. Dad used to take me to the zoo on weekends and vacations. The underwater tunnel had that exact same shimmer. We could spend hours there, Dad and I, looking at the rays and sharks swimming over our heads. Full of enthusiasm, he'd tell me about the cownose rays, how he had to feed them by hand to keep the other, faster fish from stealing their food. It was his favorite part of the day.

From the moment he shattered his knee, I saw him change from an optimistic, cheerful, hard-worker with an enormous amount of passion for his animals—to an angry, frustrated, old man who took out his misery on the government. The one thing that never changed was his love for Cross and me, and perhaps his love for Mom. I could never miss the pain in his eyes whenever her name came up, or when Cross found an old photo of her.

I hope Dad's kept himself together. I try to figure out how long he's been alone with Cross now. Has it been a month yet? It feels like an eternity. I miss them both so much it hurts.

As I think of Dad and Cross, I find myself running faster. My hand, interlocked with Frankie's, begins to sweat as I tug her forward.

"Are you thinking about him?" Frankie's soft voice snaps me out of my thoughts.

I nod. "I've missed him for so long. I really can't wait any longer. I want to hold him in my arms." Tears sting my eyes. "But I'm also worried that I might be too late. What if he's not okay?"

My mind won't stop racing. What if I've endangered Cross and Dad with my escape? What if the Guard is waiting for me at home?

"I'm sure your dad is keeping him safe. Plus, I bet your brother is just as stubborn and resilient as you are." Her finger brushes a tear from my cheek. "But running isn't safe right now. If we look too urgent, we'll draw attention to ourselves."

I gulp. "I think we should split up. I know we said we'd walk through the dunes, but if it's just the two of us, we could take a shortcut—walk south now instead of east. We'd reach Rotterdam much faster."

Frankie squeezes my hand, letting me know she heard me, though she doesn't answer right away. Instead, she sighs and bites her lower lip. "This might not be as fast, but the dunes are safer. And sticking with our group means we'll get a lot more sleep. Keeping watch one out of every four times is a lot less stressful than one out of two."

Again, I wish I'd paid better attention in school so I could better calculate how many miles it would save us to walk directly to my house from here. But the honest answer is that I have no idea. I can only trust that Frankie's making the right choice.

As the sun sets, I notice that Nora and Q are lagging quite a bit behind us. I feel my stomach contract. Should I bring it up again—that we'd be better off separating? It's inevitable that it will happen eventually, so why not now?

Frankie isn't blind—I know that. She sees the same things as me and yet says nothing. She must know what she's doing.

But instead of explaining herself, she lets go of my hand, throws her bag full of stuff in the grass and sits down, facing the water.

As she lays out the remaining sandwiches on a sweater—which serves as our picnic blanket—I plop down next to her.

"My father loves water," Frankie begins. "He always says it's what makes the Netherlands what it is, especially after all the floods our country has endured. He says the water makes us strong—that it teaches us to always be prepared, to adapt to whatever changes come." She sighs. "I used to think that was a good thing, that being strong was something to be proud of. But after my grandfather died, I learned my father's strength was anything but good. I was too young to truly understand it back then. Looking back, something changed..."

Pain pinches her voice, and I put my hand on her back, gently rubbing up and down her sweater. I can't stop thinking about her scars.

"My father lost his way somewhere. The man he is now isn't *him*. He hasn't been my father for a long time." Frankie shakes my hand off her back, her gaze still on the water.

"Humph." Nora plops down beside us. "Where do you guys get your stamina?"

"They just wanted a moment together, silly." Q grins and sits next to Nora. "Love jitters increase your adrenaline, and it's not like they can just get a room."

"Yuck." With a grossed-out expression, Nora leans away from me.

"Don't worry about it, Nora." For the first time since we sat here, Frankie takes her eyes off the water. The hard lines have dissolved from her face, giving way to a smile that radiates nothing but kindness. "It's not like that."

A hush falls over the group as everyone removes their shoes and takes food out of their bags—but my mind is anything but calm.

What does Frankie mean by it's not like that? Does she not like me the way I like her? Am I nothing more than a friend to escape with—someone to talk to and nothing more? On impulse, I run my hand over my hat, the one hiding the spiky hair beneath.

The uncertainty awakens a twisted anger within me. I *hate* that her comment has this much of an effect on my emotions. I hate that I'm acting like the kinds of girls I always judged in school. The ones who would change everything about themselves for the sake of love. I'm better than this. I didn't escape for Frankie—but for myself, Cross, and Dad. Me and my family.

As soon as the thought takes hold, I know it's not quite true. Not anymore, I suppose. I don't know when it happened, but something inside me changed. When I think of the future now, it's no longer *just* my family. The butterflies I feel for Frankie—when she smiles, when she talks to me—have grown into something bigger. Something I can't shake.

Yeah. I get it now.

I'm in love.

THIRTY-THREE

I don't say anything, but part of me is convinced that everyone has noticed how I've changed. Or maybe I've been changing for a long time, and they all noticed it before I did. Maybe the only thing different is that I see the change myself.

Three days of walking, eating and sleeping go by. I occasionally talk to Frankie, Q, and Nora—but most of the time, we walk silently together.

More and more people look sharply at us when we pass them. Despite trying to wash ourselves every night, our clothes are getting dirty and our shoes are looking worn. It's a good thing Vallance doesn't want people to know that teenagers could ever escape his *perfect* REZO facilities—otherwise, our faces would probably be plastered on every phone screen and advertising billboard. Or would they still not have caught on to our escape? Maybe our lives are so worthless that even with four wristbands going black —five, including Rhea's—and our corpses not getting sent off in the switch cell, the Guard still wouldn't bother to check on the *dead* girls bound within those walls.

Perhaps the Hangar has operated okay for so long that the threat of teenagers escaping no longer feels tangible to the Guard. But when a threat lies dormant, it's more dangerous than ever.

It's been too long. The four of us can no longer stick together.

"Let's stop here"—Q gestures to a modest lake with a playground and a public restroom nearby—"so we can refill our bottles."

Nora sighs in relief, but I can tell Frankie isn't happy about stopping.

"Come." Q grabs Nora's hand and tugs her toward the lake. "You can look after our stuff while I refill the bottles."

Once they reach the lakeside, Nora sits down and takes off her shoes and socks. Slowly, she lowers her bare feet into the cool water.

"Come here, Sin!" Nora calls. "The water is wonderful."

I smile and join her in the water. Frankie follows just a moment later—then Q, who finished refilling the bottles. Our shoes, socks, and supplies rest at the lakeside.

"Hey!" A young boy, who looks about five, wades toward us. "You guys are in my way." He gestures to our legs in the water. "I'm a water scooter and have to get past here. Mommy won't let me go any deeper than my knees. And why are you so dirty? Why do you have so little hair? I once played with scissors and cut off a piece of my hair and Mommy was very angry. But it wasn't as bad as yours. Was your mommy angry too?" The little boy prattles on and on.

"You may pass." Q steps aside and smiles at the little boy. "You know, our hairdo is a game. A very secret game. We're part of the water police. We make sure no one throws trash into the lake, but it has to be kept secret, or else we can't catch anyone. Can you keep our secret?"

The little boy nods vigorously before moving past us.

"We have to go, before he tells his mother what he saw." Frankie gets up, gathering her things and urging Q and Nora to do the same.

Is Frankie thinking the same thing? That it's finally time to split up?

My eyes widen when we pass a sign that says we're entering Wassenaar. My family used to go to the beach here often—it's a quieter town than Scheveningen, a much more touristy coastal location. That means we're about half an hour from my hometown by car, which would take several hours to trek on foot. I can't bear to keep traveling farther south, away from Rotterdam. I shouldn't be making time for this detour. I need to get home to Cross. What am I thinking?

I need to take first watch tonight. Once Q and Nora fall asleep, I'll wake Frankie, and we'll finally split up.

During dinner, when Q broaches the topic of who will stand first watch tonight, I immediately offer to do it.

"No." Frankie gives me a stern look. "You've been on guard three times in the past four days. You need to take better care of yourself. I'll take first watch."

I open my mouth to protest, but something in her gaze stops me. It doesn't really matter, anyway. I can just stay awake and talk to her. The plan doesn't change.

But once the sun is completely set, and I lay my head on a soft patch of dune grass, I know I'm not going to manage to stay awake. Frankie was right—three times in four days is too much. And soon, I feel sleep pulling me under.

I'm startled awake by a hand on my mouth. My eyes snap open, but it's only Frankie in front of me. Her blond hair stands out in tufts, and despite her stern expression, the moonlight still makes her look like an angel.

I pry her hand off my face. "What's going on?"

"We have to go." Frankie's voice is only a whisper, but her words are louder than ever.

We're in danger.

I jolt upright and look beside me. Q and Nora are awake already. Their faces have gone white, and Nora's lips are pressed into a thin line.

"I heard sirens," Frankie continues. "I'm afraid someone saw us and alerted the Guard."

I keep still and listen. While they're faint and far, I do hear sirens in the distance. My stomach turns inside out, and my hand darts to my wrist, still expecting to get zapped. I wonder when I'll shake the habit.

"We need to leave," Frankie says. "Maybe it's wiser to split up."

Nora hesitates, but Q nods. "It was bound to happen." She steps forward and pulls Frankie and me into a group hug.

"Give your little brother a big hug from me too," Q whispers in my ear.

Nora also hugs us next and presses a kiss to my cheek. "I'm gonna miss you, Sin. But we'll meet again someday, I'm sure."

I swallow the lump in my throat.

When the sirens get louder, we finally split. Tears well in my eyes, even though I've been trying to rush this very goodbye for days now.

I let Frankie lead me farther and farther away from the sirens, but as the sun slowly rises, it dawns on me that we're still not walking east, toward Rotterdam. If my instincts are right, we're actually walking down on a southbound route that cuts through the dunes. We're barely skewing off from the direction Q and Nora headed. We're not supposed to be near the dunes anymore.

When we reach a junction in the road, I purse my lips and turn east. Frankie grabs my hand and continues to guide me south.

For a moment, Rhea's words echo through my head. *"I don't like the way she looks at you. Like you're a puzzle piece."*

I try to bury the memory again, but this time, I don't succeed. The words keep bouncing through my head like Cross screaming when he has a nightmare. I can't ignore it.

"Why are we going south? I live in Rotterdam." In the back of my mind, I know my words are pointless. She's known my hometown for a long time. But still, part of me hopes that she hasn't been leading me astray—that she'll admit she made a mistake, and we'll head east from now on.

"I know someone who lives nearby. If we push ourselves for another half day, we can sleep at their place, in a real bed, take a shower, put on clean clothes, and replenish our supplies. Get some privacy." Frankie doesn't look at me. She keeps walking stubbornly.

"Once you smell me, getting some privacy will be the last thing on your mind." I try to get her to look at me with a chuckle—or at least a smile— but she continues to stare ahead.

For a few steps, I'm not sure what to say. Like a meek sheep, I follow in her trail, my thoughts whirling. Why didn't she tell me about her plan before? Why won't she look at me? Why can't I shake off Rhea's warning?

I mentally calculate how far we are from Rotterdam, and once I arrive at the same result for the third time, I yank my hand out of hers. I won't take another step until she explains herself.

"This isn't right!"

Frankie sighs and turns around. Her expression is a mix of fatigue and concern. "What's wrong?"

"If we had gone east when I first told you to, we'd have been at my home a long time ago. You talk about getting extra supplies, but if we had left at the same time as Rhea, we wouldn't need them at all. I could have held Cross in my arms by now." With each sentence, my voice gets louder, and my confidence grows.

"Sin…" Frankie tries to take my hand, but I step out of reach. "Sin, listen. I'm only doing what's best for us."

Something isn't adding up.

"I'll tell you what's best for us," I snap back. "Getting to Cross as soon as possible."

"I want that too, but…"

Something slips. Her tone changes. Something about her expression isn't quite right.

"You're lying," I mutter.

"I'm not. It's just… it's complicated."

I clench my fists. "I'm not some puzzle piece!"

She raises a brow. "Huh?"

"The way you're looking at me right now. It's like you see me as a puzzle piece, and you're trying to figure out how and where to fit me into your life." I don't even choose to use Rhea's terminology—the words naturally slip out.

"You know I love you, right?"

"Really? Because that's the first time you've said that out loud."

"I thought my actions spoke louder than words," Frankie says. "I really do love you, Sin."

Again, I hear her, but the confession feels empty. This is her final resort to get me to do what *she* wants, isn't it?

I imagine Cross sitting on the floor at home, his arms crossed in anger because it's past his bedtime and he refuses to go to sleep. Even without him by my side, he offers me a solution.

I smile. I'm done.

For a moment, hope flashes across Frankie's face.

But then I lower myself to the ground and cross my arms, mimicking Cross's rebellious posture. "I'm not taking another step until you're honest with me."

THIRTY-FOUR

Frankie chooses her words carefully—too carefully. It only makes me angrier.

"I never lied to you," she says.

"You withheld the truth."

"Sin..." Frankie looks at me pleadingly. "Don't be like that."

She extends a hand to help me up, but I glare and slap her hand away.

"Something isn't right with you. I've felt it for a while." I fold my arms again. "I pushed my feelings away because I wanted to trust you, but I can't ignore them any longer."

"I meant what I said. I know someone who lives nearby. It's only a short detour."

"From *here* it may be a small detour, but considering where we came from, it's a gigantic distance. How long have you been planning this? Since Rhea left?" I stare at her face as my words sink in. "Since we broke out of the Hangar? Before that?"

For a moment, she bears a guilty expression, but she quickly replaces it with a determined one.

A sour taste coats my tongue. "You *always* planned to come straight here from the Hangar."

"I..."

"Did you ever care about me? For even a *second*?" I finally rise to my feet. My arms are tense as I push them into my sides and clench my fists. "Was I nothing more than a tool to you?"

"Maybe at first, but..."

"When?"

A film of despair coats her face. "What?"

"When did you decide I was the easiest girl to manipulate?"

Frankie goes silent, but eventually, she sighs. "That night you talked to Q, when you mentioned your little brother and how badly you wanted to see him again."

I'm stunned she has the audacity to answer my question, to confirm that she played me for a fool. I think back to the night she speaks of—that moment when she turned over in her sleep, she wasn't asleep at all, was she? She heard everything. Even though I ended up telling her the same details later, it's still a massive invasion of privacy.

"You used Cross against me. And what for? Why drag me here?"

She struggles to get her words out.

I shake my head, losing patience, and finally storm away. I'm not wasting any more time.

"Sin, wait!"

Her words only make me walk faster.

"Sin!" Her fingers snatch my upper arm, forcing me to stop.

"I'll explain. Here." She plucks the remaining half of her Twix from our emergency bag. "This is for you."

"Are you seriously trying to bribe me with chocolate?" I knock the bar out of her hands. "There's nothing you can say that will make up for this. Nothing at all."

"Five minutes." She holds a palm up, her eyes watering. "Give me five minutes of your time. If you still want to leave after that, I'll let you go."

With a jerk, I yank my arm free—but I stay planted nonetheless.

"The Netherlands, the Party for the People, the Hangar..." Frankie swallows. "It once started as something good, as a way to provide care for the elderly in our country. Equal opportunities for every child, no matter their background. No more hunger, no more birthdays without presents. Basically, it's a good idea, I believe that."

A deep conviction echoes in her voice, but I feel only the sting of betrayal.

"Four minutes," I whisper.

"The problem with good ideas is that they're never good enough.

Change is never good enough. People always want more, until they don't see where they've crossed the line. Where does it stop? When do you accept something as good enough? I think that's where it all went wrong." Frankie stares past me. "The PFTP has lost its way. Vallance spent his entire life in his father's shadow. When his father died and he himself came to power, he crossed the line of no return. I truly believe he once wanted the best for this country. But to get what he wanted, he lost sight of the bigger picture. He ignored those who didn't fit into his image of a perfect society. And to achieve his goals, he bribed more and more people, promised more and more government positions. He wanted *more*. More money. More power. More everything."

"Why are you shit-talking Vallance when you're the bad guy here?" I ask. "Are you blind?"

"I'm not blind." Frankie continues rambling. "I don't want what Vallance wants. The Netherlands doesn't have to be perfect, but it does have to be *better*." Her bright blue eyes bore into mine. "You know that better than anyone. Your little brother can't go to school, your father can't do his job, and you yourself were sent to the Hangar. All of you are imperfect, and therefore, you don't matter. Just like me."

A tear runs down her cheek, and she abruptly wipes it away. "I'm not perfect either. Believe me. For years I tried to be. I wanted nothing more than to be perfect. Perfect for our country. Perfect for the government. Perfect for my father. But I couldn't be who he wanted me to be, no matter how hard I tried, and so I became more rebellious instead.

"When he found out I'd hacked into his computer, that was the final straw. As he unbuckled his belt, I knew I'd pushed him too far. The icy rage in his eyes told me there was no way out—he'd hit me until I couldn't get up again. So I fled. I hid for a few days, then decided I'd never submit to his whims again. I wouldn't hide from someone who'd destroyed so much."

I almost feel sympathy for her, but I push it away. She betrayed me. I don't owe her anything.

"I started to be more rebellious in public, not just with my family," Frankie continues. "The Guard caught me vandalizing a PFTP billboard during a demonstration. That's how I ended up in the Hangar. And honestly, that was probably the best way to flip my father off. His perfect daughter, part of his perfect family—arrested and locked away." She grimaces. "Of course it was all swept under the rug though. I bet he's found a way to silence the Guards who caught me."

What is she trying to tell me?

"The Guard didn't know that I'd already seen blueprints of the Hangar —that I had intel their other prisoners didn't. I decided to use that to my advantage, and come up with a plan."

I have a feeling she's not referring to her *escape from the Hangar* plan any longer. She's talking about something bigger.

Frankie takes a deep breath. "You have to understand, Sin. I need to *do* something. I can't stand by and watch the Netherlands go to the dogs any longer."

"What kind of plan?" I ask, my voice quaking. I'm not sure I even want to hear the answer. "Why *you*?"

Frankie stares at the ground as if she's hoping she'll find the right words there. Eventually, she gathers herself and looks me dead in the eye with a gaze made of ice.

"My name is Francesca Vallance. Our president is my father, and I'm going to kill him."

Do not stand by my grave and weep
I am not there
I do not sleep
I am the thousand winds that blow
I am the diamond glints in snow
I am the sunlight on ripened grain
I am the gentle autumn rain

Grateful for the end of his suffering,
But deeply mourning this loss,
We announce with heavy hearts the far too early passing of
Your intensely loved president, our husband and father,

Roger Vallance
* 24 March 2021 - † 9 May 2083

Marina Vallance
Hamilton & Lauretta
Francesca

The funeral will take place in a private ceremony on Sunday, May 12th at 12:00 p.m. in the Nieuwe Kerk in Amsterdam. Live footage will be shown at Museumplein, so the public can pay their respects.

We kindly ask you not to bring flowers, but to consider making a donation to the Roger Vallance Fund.

THIRTY-FIVE

The silence between us makes my ears ring. I can't turn back the clock. I can't undo the last minute. I can't ever again not know what I know now. I press my palms against my temples in a desperate attempt to shut out the world.

"Sin..." Frankie rests her hand on my shoulder. "Please, say something."

There are a hundred things I want to say to her, but I can't bring myself to speak.

The words reverberate through my mind. *Her father*. The man in the drawings. The one who gave her the scars on her back, the one who took her mother away from her... is our president. The man who demands harsh punishments against those who break the laws of our glorious country is breaking them himself...

I push my hands against my head even harder. Everything she told me whirls around in my head—the death of her grandfather, how it changed her father, and the pressure of always having to meet his absurdly high standards.

Pity forces my anger into the background for a second. I can't imagine what it must have been like to grow up in such a situation.

But then the anger's back. Regardless of her background, Frankie *used* me. She leveraged my love for Cross to sway me off course. She made me believe she cared about me. She gained my trust only to achieve her personal goals.

Something she said earlier comes to mind. *"If you have to do something bad to defeat someone worse—does that make you a monster?"*

These words take on a new meaning. New to me, anyway. They must have always held more weight to her. I try to remember what my reaction was back then, but my head won't cooperate.

For Frankie, at least, the answer is clear—I'm sure of that now. She doesn't care what she does or who she hurts—she's killing her monster.

Without realizing it, I start walking. Away from Frankie, away from her words. A gentle wind picks up and cools my tears.

With every step, the pressure in my head eases a little. The unstoppable cascade of thoughts starts to slow down. And bit by bit, one question gets the upper hand.

Wouldn't I do the same in her position?

As soon as the thought takes shape, a second question arises.

Wouldn't I do the same thing in *my* position? Is my position any different, even?

Frankie isn't the only one who's been oppressed. I suffered under the Vallance regime too. Life could have been so much better for my family. Maybe my upbringing was less harsh than Frankie's, but still—if we have a chance to end this, don't we owe it to our country?

I whip around and stare at Frankie. She's just a few steps behind me— she was following in my trail.

"How?" I ask.

"How what?"

"How are you going to kill him?"

"I..." Frankie balls her fists. "I don't know yet."

"You don't know yet?" The words leave my mouth in a scream. "Seriously? You've figured out how to gain my trust, make me fall in love with you, break out of a prison surveilled by countless cameras—all to kill him—but you haven't thought *that* part out? How big of an idiot could you possibly be? You break my heart and trust and for *what*?"

Her gaze burns through me. "I'm *trying*, okay? Every night, I imagine a different strategy. How I'd slip a knife between his ribs, how I'd shoot him standing in the audience during one of his speeches, how I'd wrap his own belt around his neck, and pull and pull and *pull*. But I don't know *when* I could pull any of that off. I can't just go home. He's hired security guards. He doesn't even open the door himself anymore. He'd send me right back to the Hangar—or worse. I need to get him at an unexpected time, when he feels safe." Tears extinguish the flames in her eyes. "I need to come up with something failproof."

Another doubt creeps forward from the back of my mind. "What if it's not even worth the risk? If you kill him, one of his party members could take his place and keep everything going just how it is. He'd become a martyr, a new source of inspiration for them. And if the Guard catches you, they could use your backstory to advance their narrative."

"But they'd never admit that his *daughter...*"

"Not his daughter—a crazy girl who escaped the Hangar. For all we know, they might use it as leverage to lower the minimum age for the Drain, that way they can send younger teens to that damn drill. What will you have achieved then?"

"That won't happen," she growls.

"Tell me you're not that naive. Tell me you have a contingency plan."

"I'll make sure they don't find out who's actually behind it. I can make it look like a suicide, or frame one of his guards. I can keep us safe."

"Us?" I stare right past her. "There is no *us*. Not anymore."

THIRTY-SIX

The wind feels cool against my head as I march away from Frankie. The pain hits me a second time. Every conversation, every touch, every kiss—it was all premeditated. Rhea was right. I'm just a puzzle piece to Frankie. An easy target. She tricked me into helping her escape the Hangar and survive on the run. And now she wants more?

Part of me wants to turn back and punch her in the face. How I'd love to forget, for a moment, all the self-control skills I learned from Dad. I want her to feel just a *fraction* of the pain I'm feeling right now.

But the other part of me wonders if Frankie's plan really could make a difference. Maybe, if pulled off carefully, assassinating Vallance could be a good move for the Netherlands. Maybe a replacement, even from the same party, wouldn't be as bad as him. Cross might even have a better chance at a normal life without having to live off the radar or move to another country.

Could I really handle this? Could I ignore my own feelings and help Frankie eliminate her father? I don't care what happens to her after that. If she gets busted, that's what she deserves.

I swallow the lump in my throat. I have to do this—for Cross. It's always for Cross. Forget my hurt feelings. Forget my broken heart. Forget my anger. My brother needs me. Girls like Q and Nora need me.

I turn around—and I don't have to walk far. Frankie's sitting in the tall dune grass with her head in her hands.

"We need a plan," I say, stopping in front of her.

"Sin, I..." Frankie looks up at me. Her eyes are red. "I want you to know that I really care about you."

"Without a plan, it's too risky," I reiterate, my voice breaking. I refuse to show her any more of my pain. "I've seen gambles go sideways too many times."

Frankie nods. She seems to realize that I'm not interested in resolving our problem right now. This conflict is bigger than us.

"I lived with a group nearby for a while," she says. "I hid some stuff at their place—could be helpful."

"Then... let's go there."

Frankie rises and offers a hand. "I'm glad you're coming with me, Sin."

I glance at her palm, then her face. "I need to make something clear. We don't talk about the Hangar anymore. We don't talk about the future. You don't keep things from me. And... you don't touch me."

I can tell my last demand stings, but she agrees nonetheless. "Let's focus on my father. His end is our new beginning."

I nod. Our new beginning—*our* meaning Cross, Dad, and me. I know Frankie includes herself in my *our*, but that ship has sailed.

We spend the first few hours in silence, for the most part. She only talked to me twice—once to say that she had to pee and another when she found a lost backpack in the grass. The 100-guilder bill in its side pocket will make sure we won't sleep hungry tonight.

Only when we reach the city limits of The Hague does Frankie clear her throat. "It's still over an hour's walk to my friend's place. I suggest we get something to eat first."

I nod. Frankie stops at a cafeteria and looks at me questioningly. "Fries?"

My stomach rumbles at the thought of hot, unhealthy food. "Don't they know your face here?"

"I grew up on the other side of town, and my father would never let me eat in this kind of run-down place."

Before I can protest, Frankie steps inside.

A few minutes later, she's back with a huge paper bag of food and a cardboard holder with two sodas. "Fries, cheese nuggets, mayo, and more fries." With a smile, she holds the bag out in front of me. "Enjoy your meal."

When I bite into a cheese nugget, I can't suppress a groan. The hot cheese burns my tongue, but its soft, salty taste makes up for it. When was the last time I ate something fried?

"Tasty, right?" Frankie grabs a handful of fries and a packet of mayonnaise from the bag. One by one, she dips the fries into the sauce and eats them. "My father reckoned it was bad for his reputation if he was caught eating unhealthy food. A healthy mind in a healthy body was one of his many mantras. My mom used to smuggle us junk food sometimes."

I watch Frankie wander down memory lane. Little laugh lines appear by her eyes.

"All those nights I snuck out of the house, I always went to fast food places first. How about you?"

I continue eating, refusing to answer her question. It doesn't feel right to give her more information about my private life. I won't allow her to manipulate any more of me.

Frankie slides the bag my way. "You want the other cheese nuggets too?"

I know I should turn down her offer, that this is probably just a courtesy call. But whatever—I don't care. I nod, grab the leftover snacks from the bag and take a big bite. The cheese runs in long strands from the nugget down my chin.

Grinning, Frankie takes a napkin out of the bag and lifts it to wipe away the cheese.

I jerk away from her. "I'm not some toddler."

"No, I know. I just wanted to..."

"Why did you do it?" I snap.

She gives me a puzzled look.

"Why did you need me? You could have dug that hole by yourself or gone your own way after the Hangar. Why did you have to involve me?"

She answers like I asked the easiest question in the world. "I couldn't do it alone, actually. All of you would have seen me scraping at that wall in plain sight. Plus, it would have taken much longer."

I roll my eyes.

"But the more I got to know you, the more I liked you. Really, I fell in love with you. And I *still* want to be with you."

"Stop." I turn my head away. "I don't want to hear it."

Frankie's shoulders slump. We eat and drink in silence until we're down to the last crumb.

"We should go." She sounds tired.

Without sparing me a glance, Frankie gets up and wads up our trash. I watch her walk away and throw everything in a bin. It's almost like I can see the scars right through the fabric of her T-shirt, each mark screaming that she's had a hard enough time as it is, that I shouldn't be this cold to her. That she doesn't deserve this. That I'm being a bitch.

No, I refuse to listen to the voice in my head. I refuse to feel guilty.

She made her own choices; I'm making mine.

THIRTY-SEVEN

We walk farther and farther into The Hague. The houses here are huddled together, and the asphalted streets give way to dark cobblestones.

Every house proudly flies the Dutch flag, adorned with golden streamers that glimmer in the light of the setting sun. I wonder what it looked like back when streamers were still orange. After the King was forced to step down, our orange pennants were soon replaced by the golden variety. It was the color that best suited our country—the perfect, golden Netherlands.

I shift my gaze from the flags to the cobblestones below, watching my feet as I walk.

How long will it take to reach Frankie's friends?

How long will it take to plot, prepare, and execute the attack?

How long will it take for me to hold Cross again?

Frankie turns down a narrow side street, casting a glance over her shoulder. I have no idea if she's checking to see if I'm following her—or checking to see if anyone's following *us*. Whichever it is, she seems satisfied and keeps walking.

Three more alleyways later, she suddenly comes to a halt.

Wooden partitions stand out against a wall of red bricks. Frankie looks over her shoulder before sliding the wooden partitions aside. The hole beneath it must have once belonged to a storage hatch; a way to fill the basement below with wine, or cheese, or anything else that was plentiful.

Hesitantly, Frankie extends her hand, but before I can decide whether I want to take it, she lowers it again. She steps aside and gestures for me to go first.

"It's not that deep, but the ground's uneven, so I wouldn't jump. There are rungs you can hold on to as you make your way down."

I do as she says and lower myself feet-first into the hole. I feel around with my toes until I find the first rung, then start my descent.

My eyes have to get used to the dark before I can take in the space. I'm standing in a basement that measures at least seven feet in each direction. Wooden crates are stacked against one of the walls, and there's a door directly in front of me.

I look up again and see Frankie's feet appear. She slides the partitions into place to cover our entrance, and the sliver of light coming in disappears.

I can't see anything—all I hear is Frankie joining me on the ground.

"Sin?" Frankie whispers.

I feel her fingertips brush along my upper arm, and goosebumps erupt across my skin. I hold my breath and wait for her to remove her hand.

"We have to keep going." Her words are close to my ear. "Can you see enough to follow me?"

I blink a few times. Slowly but surely, I discern her silhouette. "Yeah. Where should we go? And where are we?"

"This is where I used to sleep whenever I ran away. It's a shelter for anyone who doesn't want to, or can't function, within the system. We help each other where necessary, and it's dry and safe here. Outside, you always run the risk of being caught by the Guard."

Frankie leads the way, looking over her shoulder every few seconds to see if I'm still following her.

"Riff is the one in charge here. His parents used to own a restaurant right above us—that's how he knew about this place. Once my father tightened the restrictions on selling meat, they could no longer afford rent and moved. Riff has managed to keep the cellar open. The corridor system down here is centuries old. The center of national power has been in The Hague for hundreds of years, and these underground tunnels were constructed to get the Netherlands' leaders out safely in the event of an attack, a very long time ago. Most have collapsed, but some are now used as living and sleeping quarters."

Only when Frankie is silent for a moment do I hear the quiet sounds in the tunnel: the gentle dripping of water, car tires on the asphalt above our heads, and very distantly, the murmur of people talking.

"And you're sure that Riff can be trusted?"

A wry laugh escapes her. "I'm sure he *can't* be trusted."

"What?"

"Riff has only one goal—to make sure things go well for himself and the people in his care. He won't betray us, though. He's a victim of the system too. He hates Vallance as much as I do, and that creates a bond."

I realize that I've never heard her call the president *Dad*.

"We're safe here, for now," Frankie continues.

The tunnel's stone walls become coarser and more uneven as we travel deeper. The mortar is swept away, partly by footsteps and partly by time. It's clear this underground corridor is much older than the basement we came from.

Dad would have loved this, back in the day. He could talk for hours about the tunnels that different animals burrowed, and how we as humans could learn something from them.

With every step, the sound of conversations in the distance grows louder. I hear someone laughing, followed by a growl.

I stiffen at the sound. For all we know, Riff was arrested a while ago. We could be walking right into a trap set up by the Guard.

"Don't worry. As long as Riff's goals aren't the same as ours, he'd never do anything to help the government." Frankie sets a hand on my shoulder. "But just to be safe, I think it's best if we don't tell him where we came from."

I shrug Frankie's hand off. "Why not?"

A *click* makes me flinch, and I feel something cold against the back of my head.

My body petrifies, and my heart pounds against my ribs.

"Yeah, Frankie." The man's voice is cold and cynical. "Whyever not?"

FROM OUR ARCHIVES:
Death of president shocks nation

From your interim president Hamilton Vallance

It is with great pain that I address you as interim president of the Netherlands. The passing of my father has touched us all deeply, and I know that you, like me, will need time to come to terms with this loss.

During the last days of his brief illness, my father expressed his wish that I, as his heir, continue his work. I know this is not the way a leader typically comes to power. Therefore, my first action will be to organize a referendum in which the people can decide on this.

In the meantime, however, I will not be idle, because my father would not have wanted that. As he always said, "We have come a long way, but we can always make our country more successful, and more beautiful."

Together we are stronger. Choose PFTP!

For more information, or to donate to the Roger Vallance Fund, click here!

93,221 shares

THIRTY-EIGHT

My knees buckle. The temperature in the tunnel suddenly seems to drop below freezing.

"You know what? Don't answer that yet," the man continues. "Why don't you turn around and put your hands above your head, flat against the wall?"

I comply, pressing my trembling palms to the cold stones. Fingers slip down my body, across my arms, into the elastic band of my pants before they trail further down between my legs and ankles. I bite my lip and let it happen.

"They're clean," a second voice says.

"Take them to the hall."

The first man pins my arms behind me, and the second does the same to Frankie. We're frogmarched into a large room with torches on the wall that cast everything in an eerie orange glow. Clusters of people stand along the outskirts of the hall. Five, twelve—at least twenty stare at us with looks that alternate between suspicion and curiosity.

The men let go of Frankie and me once we're in the middle of the room. We have no weapons and are far outnumbered. We are not a threat to them.

Hesitantly, I look at Frankie, who casually plops onto a chair. I remain standing.

"It's been a while, Frankie. We thought you'd abandoned us." The frosty voice belongs to the man who found us in the tunnel—a tall, skinny guy with a flaxen beard. Glasses balance on the tip of his nose, stern green eyes staring through them. His black pants are covered in smudges, yet his shirt looks ironed.

"I would never leave you behind, Riff." Frankie sounds calm, but she's talking slower than usual. I can tell she's weighing each word carefully.

"Aren't you gonna introduce us to your friend with the unusual haircut?" Riff cocks his head at her, then me. "It's a little suspicious, how it perfectly matches yours. Almost looks like the buzzcut they give girls in the Hangar."

"You have no idea what you're talking about, Riff." Frankie gestures to me. "This is Sin. Her blond curls stood out too much, so we figured we'd just cut her hair off. I ended up doing the same. If people see us from a distance and think we're guys, who cares? Certain things are easier if you don't stand out."

I try to keep a straight face. *Blond curls?* My short, spiky hair could be called *light brown* if you're being generous.

"And what kind of things would be easier, hmm?"

"What do *you* care?"

The two stare each other down, until eventually, Riff breaks a grin. "Let me hear from this friend of yours." His gaze shifts to me, and only now do I see his green eyes up close. It looks like someone has punctured them to make the black of his pupils bleed into his irises. "Tell me—why are you here with good old Frankie?"

His gaze holds me hostage, and I know he won't accept silence.

"It's safer in a pair than alone," I reply.

Riff laughs, looking back at Frankie. "Well, from the sound of it, your story isn't as romantic as I thought. Why don't you tell me why you're back?"

"I needed a place to sleep," Frankie says.

"All of a sudden? After all those weeks we didn't hear from you? You don't call, you don't write... How can we trust you?"

"You know we have nothing on us. And besides—two against twenty wouldn't be a very fair fight, would it?"

"I suppose not," he says.

"And you know I don't make bad choices for the sake of self-preservation."

I snicker at her final line. I can't help it.

Riff chuckles too. "Yes, I know that, and apparently your girlfriend does too."

I drop my smile. "My name is Sin." This Riff guy is starting to get on my nerves.

"Very well. Sin." He pronounces my name slowly, as if testing the letters on his tongue for the first time. "Can you confirm what Frankie says? That you're just looking for a place to sleep?"

I nod. "Just one night, and we'll be out of your hair."

I have nothing to stick around for, after all.

THIRTY-NINE

"You'll have to share a bed. We don't have much extra room, but judging by the way you look at her, Frankie, I don't think you'll have a problem with that." Riff turns to me and chuckles, giving me a slow once-over. Then he lowers his voice, like it's just between us. "But if Frankie makes you uncomfortable, you can always sleep in my bed."

"No thank you," I say dryly.

Riff raises both palms. "Just an offer." He turns back to Frankie. "Your stuff's still in your old place. And you're just in time—we were about to clear it for someone else."

Frankie shrugs. "Right. Impeccable timing. Come." She grabs my hand and pulls me toward the other side of the hall. Everyone's eyes are following me.

We travel down a narrow tunnel, where hanging LEDs occasionally illuminate the way. The ceiling gets lower the farther we go. I have to walk the last few feet hunched over to keep from hitting my head.

"Here it is." Frankie points to an opening in the tunnel wall and pulls me into it. The room is small—seven by seven feet at the most—but the ceiling is high enough for me to stand up straight. A ray of light from the hallway barely illuminates a mat and a backpack on the floor.

The walls are made of stones, some pieces missing. Frankie leans over and reaches into one of the gaps. I hear her exhale in relief before she pulls something out.

It's a shoebox. She opens the lid to reveal a shiny pistol on a bed of black velvet. Crammed underneath the gun is a stack of bills.

"It's still here." Frankie tucks the box into the backpack, plops down on the middle of the mat, and gestures for me to sit next to her.

I almost hesitate, but my legs are too tired. Still, I leave as much space between us as possible.

"Sin, I want to…" Frankie starts, but I don't let her finish.

"What's the plan? We leave here tomorrow. Then what?"

Frankie leans in and whispers. "Tomorrow could be our day. It's the annual summer march. My father will be delivering a speech at the Binnenhof."

"Seriously? You want to make an attempt while he's surrounded by the Guard?" I raise a brow. "That sounds logical."

"I've been to these marches before, okay? There won't be too many Guard members there—it'd make my father look paranoid, and he hates showing fear. Plus, there's always this moment, right before he does his speech, when he's completely alone. That's our cue."

My same worry resurfaces. I'm not sure about this anymore.

"Suppose we succeed," I say. "Will *you* take his place as president?"

"This isn't some book we're in, Sin. This isn't a story where a couple of teenagers overthrow the government, and everything magically gets better. This is *not* a revolution. I just want to get on with my life, and I can't while he's around."

I don't respond. I just let her words settle. Maybe she's right. My priority is my family—and for the first time, maybe even myself. Maybe I don't need to worry about what happens to the Netherlands after the assassination, so long as I protect Cross. Whoever the next president is, I'll be there for my brother.

"You can use the mat." Frankie seems to take my silence as a sign that our conversation is over. "I'll sleep on the floor." She slides off the mat and settles on the ground.

Despite everything, it hurts—the fact that she's not even trying anymore. I lie down and turn my back to her. What does it even matter?

I hear her deep breaths and feel her gaze against my back.

I squeeze my eyes shut. I'm tired and just want to sleep for a few hours.

"Sin?"

Frustrated, I roll over to face her. "*What*?"

"I..." Frankie toys with the hems of her sleeves. "I want you to know that you're free to go."

"Was there ever a time I *wasn't*?"

"Of course you were, but..." Frankie sighs. "I know you want to see Vallance's reign come to an end, but I don't want to drag you deeper into this. You can still get away. See Cross again."

I know she means well, but her words leave my blood boiling. I need to see this through. If I don't help, Frankie might do something stupid and get caught.

"I'm finishing what I started," I say.

Hurt flashes across her face. "It's your choice. But if panic breaks out, make sure you flee. I don't want you taking the fall with me."

"And you?" I know I'm being antagonistic, but underneath the rage, there's still a remnant of what we once had. Love, or infatuation—I'm not sure. But either way, it glues me here. I can't seem to let go of her.

Frankie doesn't hesitate. "I'll pull the trigger. I don't care what happens next."

From your president Hamilton Vallance

A country in which everyone makes a positive contribution. A country in which we take care of each other. A country that rewards those who do their best for our nation.

It was my father's dream—and I am convinced that together, we can achieve it.

Unfortunately, news has spread of individuals trying to sabotage this dream. People who want to take advantage of you and your loved ones to destroy everything we have worked for.

We will not let this happen! Only by cutting out the rotten apples in society can people like you and me live the life we deserve.

We are starting today! Together we are stronger. Choose PFTP!

For more information, or to donate to the Roger Vallance Fund, click <u>here</u>!

FORTY

In a strange way, this feels like her final goodbye. Frankie and I both know that if she pulls the trigger on Vallance, her chances of getting away in the ensuing chaos are close to none. It's not fair, but I can't help but realize that she's always chosen vengeance over her feelings for me—whatever those feelings are. She's always been willing to endanger herself at the cost of a future with me.

My eyes sting. I roll onto my back and bite my lip, staring at the ceiling. Soon, my cheeks are wet with tears I can't hold back.

"Sin..." Frankie's voice is soft and close. She puts a hand on my shoulder, forcing me to turn toward her again.

My eyes brim with tears as I move to lie next to her on the floor. "Be honest. Did I ever mean anything to you?"

She sighs. "You mean more to me than I want to admit. More than I *dare* to admit. I always kept people at a distance out of fear of getting hurt, and I intended to do the same with you. Yes, I tried to get close to you so you'd help with my escape plan, but once I knew you, I couldn't push you away anymore. In the Hangar, for the first time in my life, I was comfortable letting someone in. I love you, Sin. Much more than you realize."

Frankie puts her hand on my cheek and leans in. When her soft lips touch mine, the hairs on my arms stand on end. Her hand slides from my cheek to my neck and she pulls me closer. Gently, her fingers caress my neck, my hairline. Butterflies dance in my stomach as our faces collide.

I don't want this. Or do I? Can I indulge in this kiss without getting even more emotionally attached to her? Can I choose this, simply because I'm stressed, and tired, and would really like to feel good right now?

I choose to lose myself in her kiss. In her touch. Just for this moment, I let my fear of losing her trump my resentment. My tongue finds hers and my body sets on fire. I've missed her.

But when she pulls her head back, my thoughts turn cloudy again. This is the same girl who is about to commit murder, no matter the consequences for her—or me.

"You need to get away," I declare.

Hope flashes in her eyes again, but my reasoning is different than she expects.

"What do you think would happen if you get caught? The Guard will figure out who you are and check the Hangar. Then they'll know for certain that other girls escaped too. They'll be on our case even more than they already are—and they know where our families live. This decision affects more than just you." I want to add the part she wants to hear—that I can't lose her—but I don't.

Frankie swallows hard. "You're right. I can't get caught. For you... and the other girls." A pause. "Why don't you get to sleep? Tomorrow's a big day." She presses another kiss to my lips and rolls onto her other side.

I turn so we're lying back to back, and close my eyes.

Frankie already got everything from me that she needed. And yet, she's still trying to be close to me. Could it be that she swayed me into coming here instead of Rotterdam because she simply wanted to keep me around? Because she wasn't ready to say goodbye? Is it foolish to want that to be true?

"Sin."

"Yeah?"

"I know that kiss doesn't fix anything. I know you're still mad at me. But I did everything with an important purpose in mind."

I face her again with a sigh. "I know. I just wish I was part of that purpose —that you'd consider me in your plans too."

Frankie's fingers wrap around mine. "You deserve that. You deserve *more*. Someone who can give you everything, but that's not me. Not yet, at least.

I can't spend the rest of my life looking over my shoulder just because I'm afraid he'll find me."

I hesitate to ask the question. "Where are you going to shoot from?"

"I have a way to get close. But I don't want you worrying about that." Frankie trails a fingertip from my forehead down to my cheek, then my chin. "You should really try to sleep."

After everything we've said, she still doesn't trust me. Just like she did in the Hangar, she's hiding bits and pieces of her plan—not showing me the full picture.

FORTY-ONE

When I wake up, the spot beside me is cold. I rise, looking for Frankie.

In a small, makeshift kitchen, two men stand by a large pan, stirring something that looks like oatmeal.

As I draw closer, one of them smiles, gesturing to a table of food. I offer a grateful nod, grab an apple and a piece of cheese, and continue my search, eating on the way.

Finally, I find Frankie in the hallway where we entered the tunnels yesterday. She sits with her back against the wall, staring blankly ahead.

"Hey."

She glances over, her eyes widening.

"They're handing out oatmeal. If you're quick enough…" I trail off when I notice her startled expression. "Are you okay?" I lower myself and sit next to her.

Frankie nods. She's quiet for a moment before she says, "I can't believe the time has finally come. I've been looking forward to this for so long, but… I just… I don't know. Is it stupid for me to have doubts right now?"

"Of course not. You can still back out. You don't owe anything to anyone."

"I don't have doubts about *that*. I want him dead."

I study her expression, but I can't read why she's conflicted. "Then what *do* you have doubts about?"

"Whether it's a good idea to let you tag along today. It probably won't change anything—I bet it won't affect how scared I am. I just wish I could look into the future and be sure that something will have changed by the time we wake up tomorrow. Part of me is afraid of making everything worse, especially for you."

No one can tell the future, but I get what she means. How many times have I wished I could do exactly that? When you face a difficult choice, the consequences of which you can't see, how do you make the right choice? I'm sure Dad wouldn't have left Cross unregistered, had he known the consequences. Mom leaving, me being sent off to the Hangar... everything would have turned out differently.

Deep down, I know there's no point in thinking about choices already made. Dad once told me that a cheetah will lie for hours, waiting for suitable prey. Once it chooses a target, it can't undo it. Like an arrow from a bow, the cheetah flies at its prey. It has a maximum of sixty seconds to catch it before overheating. Doubt, in this case, means hunger.

Dad always thought people should be more like cheetahs. *Make a choice and go for it*, he'd say. *There is no turning back.*

"You already decided what to do," I conclude. "Now you need to lock in. If you hesitate, we'll have nothing to eat."

"Huh?" Frankie gives me a puzzled look.

"It's an analogy my father used to make," I explain. "Once doubt sets in, things tend to go wrong. Do it or don't, but never halfway."

Frankie manages a weak smile. "I hope I can meet your father someday."

I bite my lip. Do I want her to? I know it's diametrically opposed to everything I just said, but I don't want to make a decision yet about a possible future with her.

Frankie changes the subject. "When the time comes, I don't want you sticking around for me. I want you to leave and hide. Don't trust anyone. I'll do my best to escape, and I'll come to the fast food joint where we got those cheese nuggets. You can wait for me there, and if I don't show up, leave without me." She pulls out a thick stack of guilders out of her pocket. "This can get you to Rotterdam."

I take the money and gawk at it. There must be at least a thousand guilders —enough to take a bus, train, or even a cab. I won't have to walk anymore.

"I hope one day you'll be able to forgive me."

Now I'm biting my lip again. It sounds so simple—forgiving her, trusting her. Dad's words about the cheetah come back to me. Not making a choice means starvation. This could be the last time I'm able to talk to Frankie. My last chance to give her the gift of *I forgive you*.

But I can't say the words she wants to hear. Not yet.

Softly, Frankie rises to her feet. "It's time."

FORTY-TWO

For the summer march, the Binnenhof's courtyard is decorated with a temporary stage in the middle, hundreds of orange-and-gold signs, and Dutch flags hanging from every easel. Civilians form a massive crowd that constantly moves, everyone pushing and shoving in hopes of catching a better view of the president once he appears.

Vallance is supposed to walk between two rows of Guard members that are already lined up on the stage. They're technically part of the summer march to display the government's respect for the military, but in actuality, they're here to nip any sign of disorder in the bud. I notice they have rifles at the ready.

Frankie pulls me along, leading me to an area behind the stage. After we said goodbye to Riff and left for the Binnenhof, we barely spoke, though she held my hand the whole time. It felt uncomfortable at first, but right now, I'm glad she's clutching my hand—otherwise I would have lost her in this crowd a long time ago.

She stops at a marquee made of white tarp that's been set up for Vallance —a private area for him to review his speech one last time after the march. A young Guard member stands at the entrance to the tent. The president's sigil, two intersecting capital *V*s, is embroidered on his breast pocket in gold thread, marking him as one of Vallance's personal guards.

Next to him, an older, bald guard stands with his back to us. When the young guard whispers something to him, he walks away with long strides.

"So... this is goodbye." Frankie puts her hands on my upper arms and gives me a piercing look. "Get far away from here, okay? It'll be at least twenty minutes before my father shows face. Use that time to put as much distance between us as possible, so they'll never know you were involved. Now hurry—the other guard will be back any minute."

I can't read any emotions on her face. No regret, no sadness. It's like our goodbye doesn't affect her at all.

I have no clue what to say to her, what I *want* to say. Before I can decide on the words, she's gone, already creeping alongside the white canvas of the marquee, toward the young man standing guard. I hold my breath when she reaches for him.

Gently, she puts her hand on his neck and turns his face, pressing a kiss to the corner of his lips—like she meant to kiss him on the cheek, but pleasantly missed.

The man's eyes sparkle, and he wraps his hands around Frankie's waist.

I avert my gaze. Jealousy scratches against my chest like a caged tiger. I have to keep myself from running after them and pushing him off her.

When I look back at them, they're whispering to each other. The man puts something in Frankie's hands, and she darts inside, disappearing between the tent flaps.

My legs go weak. Will this be the last time I see her?

No. I refuse to flee while she plays a role that could completely change *my* future.

The guard stares at the stage for a while, but I can tell from the look in his eyes that he's still thinking about Frankie's kiss.

I look around. There are two cameras on the corners of the marquee. If I avoid their directions, I should be able to get into the tent unseen. It's a pretty delicate structure—nothing like the Hangar's walls. If I broke through one of *those*, I can get through this.

I turn the corner to the side of the tent, out of the guard's view. Then I drop to my knees and crawl, hoping the crowd's distracting enough for no one to notice me. My heart is beating in my throat as I slide underneath the tent canvas, flat on my belly.

I pop up behind a white leather couch. I keep my head down and observe the tent's interior.

Despite its temporary structure, it looks like a luxurious living room in here. Across from the couch is a chair with matching leather upholstery. On a coffee table between them sits a microphone, a glass of white wine, and a bowl of brightly colored candies. The other side of the tent has a clothes rack filled with almost identical white jackets and a vanity desk with various types of makeup. Everything is perfect for the few sparse minutes our president will spend inside this tent.

Frankie is pacing with her hands folded around something small and black. The pistol.

I hesitate to let her know I'm here and duck my head behind the couch again. I'll stay here for another ten minutes, to give her some space to think alone, and then I'll emerge. We're going to do this together. I'm here to help.

I focus on my breathing and try to stay calm. Even without looking at Frankie, I can feel her tension in the air. Her stress is contagious.

Suddenly, voices from outside pipe up, and Frankie stops pacing.

"There was a disruption on the way here." The speaker's voice is unmistakably clear from inside our thin tent walls.

The crowd goes silent.

"The perpetrators have been dealt with, but we've asked the parade to walk faster. The president will be here in three minutes."

I need to let her know I'm here.

I rise, but immediately drop back to the floor when I hear the tent flap open.

Frankie darts behind the rack of clothes—just in time.

A man with slick, jet-black hair sprints into the marquee and rushes to the vanity. He twists the caps off makeup bottles and arranges a few brushes. Then he pulls out the chair and stands behind it with folded hands, waiting to assist the president.

I hear voices again, many more this time. I immediately recognize the louder voice.

"This is clearly the work of organized criminals!"

Vallance is right outside this tent.

The flap is pushed aside, and there he is—the president of the Netherlands.

The man I've seen on TV for years. The man who single-handedly destroyed our country in his drive for *more*, for *better*, for *perfect*. The man who caused the scars on Frankie's back.

"We need to find them," Vallance finishes.

A guard quickly follows him in. "Absolutely, sir."

"Has everyone in the audience been checked?"

"Of course, sir."

"Make sure the extra surveillance stays out of sight."

"Yes, sir."

"Go," he orders, and the guard complies.

Extra surveillance?

The words echo through my head, and I shoot a nervous glance at the clothing rack that Frankie is hiding behind. She didn't factor *extra surveillance* into her plan.

"What a day," Vallance mumbles, trudging over to the coffee table. Now it's just him and the slick-haired makeup artist by the vanity—or so he thinks.

I'm too scared to move. From my hiding place, I watch Vallance pick up the wine glass, only to set it down empty two seconds later.

"What a day," he repeats in a pensive voice. He plucks a green candy from the bowl.

The flap of the tent opens again, and a man wearing a headset peeks in. "Mr. President, we are ready for you."

Vallance sighs. "Five more minutes."

"Excellent, sir." The man disappears.

Finally, Vallance walks to the vanity desk and plops onto the chair. Without speaking, the slick-haired makeup artist grabs a tube and spreads pale pink cream across the president's face.

"I'll use darker makeup on you today, sir. The clouds will make your complexion pale under all those lights."

Vallance closes his eyes.

That's when the clothing rack judders.

With her pistol pointed at Vallance, Frankie steps out from behind the white jackets.

FORTY-THREE

The gun trembles in Frankie's outstretched hands, and the makeup artist gasps.

Vallance opens his eyes. For a moment, confusion flashes across his face —but then he grins.

"Francesca. I didn't know you were back already. What a surprise."

Frankie's lower lip quivers, and deep lines crease the corners of her mouth.

"Put that thing away, will you? Say what you have to say and I'll listen, but we both know you don't have the guts to shoot your own father."

"I've changed." Frankie's voice is much higher than usual. "I won't be oppressed anymore."

"Oppressed? My dear child, what's gotten into your head? I'm your father. You *have* to obey me. It's the natural order." Vallance slowly rises to face Frankie. He's over a foot taller than her, and he looks sharp in his smart, white suit.

"Don't come any closer." The pistol shakes even more. "I really will do it, you know."

"And then what?" Vallance puts his hands in the air—a mocking surrender —and takes a step toward her. "What do you think this will accomplish, Francesca? After all the grief you caused your mother with this rebellious streak of yours, you've practically taken away her only daughter. Do you really want to take away her beloved husband as well?"

"I... You..." Frankie stumbles over her words, the color draining from her face.

"You're weak, Francesca. I tried my best to toughen you up, to prepare you as my successor, but clearly, I failed. You have too much of your mother's genes in you."

"Don't talk about Mom like that." Her eyes well up, but she still doesn't pull the trigger.

Vallance takes another step.

I have to do something.

Through the corner of my eye, I see the makeup artist shuffle toward the tent flap. If he slips out, he'll alert the Guard.

It's now or never.

"Then shoot me, Francesca. Show me I was wrong, that you *are* strong." Another step. "Prove me wrong. Prove that I did not father a coward. Prove that you are better than your mother."

"I *hate* you." Frankie's words are a mere whisper, but the gunshot that resounds is deafening.

The makeup artist dives away, his mouth opening in a soundless scream. He stumbles into one of the poles that holds up the marquee.

The tarp topples over like a heavy blanket, shoving me down onto my stomach. My ears ring. Everything is white. I force myself up until I'm on my hands and knees, and I crawl in Frankie's direction. The glass coffee table has shattered—infinite shards litter the floor, and the brightly colored candies scatter among them like confetti.

I keep crawling, trying to avoid the glass, but a few pieces prick my palms anyway.

When my hand lands in a pool of something warm and sticky, a shiver travels down my spine. It's too much blood to be mine. But who does it belong to then? I can't shake the fear that while I was focused on the makeup artist, Vallance could have stolen Frankie's pistol. Or maybe he had a gun of his own—is that why he was acting so confident?

The pungent smell of feces and urine fills the tent, forcing me to breathe through my mouth.

A tremendous commotion is audible outside the marquee. Angry screams, shots, followed by more screams—this time of agony.

There. Right in front of me, a hand pokes out from under the white tarp.

To my relief, it's too big to be Frankie's.

I gulp and keep crawling, then glance back at the wide eyes of our president. Blood flows from a gaping wound in his neck. Fast, then slow. Faster, slower. He is breathing. He is still alive.

A quiet growl emerges from his mouth. He lifts his hand slightly off the ground—reaching out to me for help.

I slap his hand down. I have to find Frankie.

Vallance groans, his eyes rolling back in their sockets. I leave him behind.

Since the Guard is close, I can't risk calling her name and drawing attention to myself, so I keep crawling under the canvas, heading in the direction I saw her in earlier.

"Over here!" A heavy, male voice comes from right behind me. "The president has been shot!"

I crawl faster. Someone fires a gun again. A dull *thud* nearby lets me know that someone close has been shot. I'm right in the middle of the action.

I have to get out of here.

I see an area with more leeway under the tarp ahead. The fabric is partly propped up by the dressing table and clothing rack.

Finally, I find her.

Frankie is on her knees, her hands still folded around the pistol. Tears run down her pale face.

"You did it, Frankie," I say quietly, shuffling toward her on my knees. "You shot him."

She blinks slowly. I'm not sure if she registered what I just said. I come a little closer and gently guide her hands—and the pistol trapped in them —away from me.

"You did it," I repeat.

She still won't meet my gaze. She must be in shock.

"Listen." My voice is firmer now. "It's not over yet. We need to get out of here. Now, okay? Follow me."

Thankfully, she does. We crawl in the opposite direction of the stage, away from the shouting, even though it requires more time under this humid tarp.

Once we finally get out, Frankie scrambles to her feet. Her eyes are bright and focused again. She readjusts her grip on the pistol and studies the opposite direction of the courtyard. I do the same. In the distance, I see trees and army trucks that belong to the Guard. Among them is a mobile toilet truck. If we can make it there, we can hide in the toilet section.

Frankie notices the same thing. With her free hand, she grabs my wrist, and we race for the trucks, cutting through everyone else that's fleeing in this direction.

We stay close. We make it to the trees.

I try to open the door to the toilet area, but it's locked. Frankie and I press our backs against the side of the truck and silently regroup.

Think, I tell myself. *Where should we go now?*

I flinch when the toilet truck rumbles behind me. Someone's actually inside.

Frankie whips around and points her gun at the door.

It opens, and the man who steps out quickly raises both hands. It's that same guy—the young guard who let Frankie into the marquee.

He looks from the gun to Frankie and lets out a sigh, lowering his hands. "Thank God you're safe. I heard the shots and didn't know..." He trails off, then simply wraps his arms around her. She hugs him back. It just now occurs to me that they must know each other. A single kiss couldn't possibly convince him to let her into that tent.

"I did what you told me to," the guard says. "I made sure I was alone, and then I hid. But we have to get away now. It's only a matter of time before they suspect me."

When he pulls away from her, his eyes catch mine. "Who's this?"

"A friend," Frankie says. "Now Jonah, focus. Do you have a car?"

"Yeah, a little further down."

"There, with the buzz cut!" A shrill voice rings out from the direction we came from. "She's the shooter!"

It's the president's makeup artist. His hands are tied behind his back, and his face is bright red. Two guards hold his arms with death grips.

"I told you it wasn't me! I told you there was someone else! She knew him. She—"

A bullet cuts him off. The makeup artist collapses.

My eyes widen as I face Jonah. He's holding his Guard-issued rifle.

Frankie pushes me forward and grabs Jonah by the arm. We sprint away from the two guards after us, darting around trees and army trucks.

More shots ring out. A bullet strikes a tree trunk right next to my head. Every few yards, Jonah and Frankie turn around to fire shots back. They don't hit anyone, but at least it slows our chasers down.

"Here, on the left!" Jonah calls. "The red car behind that van."

"Hurry, your keys!" Frankie yells.

As soon as he pulls them out of his pocket, Frankie snatches them. The car beeps when she presses the button on the key fob

"Get inside," she tells me.

I open the door and slide into the passenger seat. Frankie gets behind the wheel.

"Stop!" one of the guards yells. He's not far from our car. "You're under arrest!"

Jonah's still outside. He aims his rifle and shoots the first guard down. The other one raises his gun, aiming back at Jonah. They have each other in check.

A scream lodges in my throat when I hear Jonah cry out. He doubles over and sinks to his knees, right outside his car.

"No!" Frankie screams. Tears spill from her eyes—but the guard who shot Jonah is still after us, and she knows it isn't the time to grieve. She rams the keys into the ignition and hits the gas.

The acceleration pushes me back against the leather upholstery, and I fasten my seatbelt with trembling hands.

The car makes a sharp turn. My cheek slams into the window. From the corner of my eye, I see Jonah sprawled out on the grass, completely immobile.

Frankie focuses on the road ahead with a pale, strained face. Her knuckles turn white as she squeezes the wheel. Her pistol is in her lap.

"I've done it." She wipes the tears from her cheeks. "I've really done it."

FORTY-FOUR

We zip down the road at full speed. It's quiet. Frankie hasn't spoken since we fled the Binnenhof. I'm not sure what to say either.

Jonah's car doesn't have a clock, so I can't tell how long we've been on this road. I know we're not in the downtown part of The Hague anymore, which is good. There's no high-rise buildings anymore—just one-story houses in the suburbs.

With a jerk, Frankie pulls over and stops the car. She tucks the pistol into the waistband of her pants, drapes the hem of her T-shirt over it, and beckons for me to get out with her.

"It's only a matter of time before the Guard realizes that Jonah's car is gone. We need another means of transportation." She leads me down the sidewalk. "I've been in this area before. We can grab a Sharewheels a few blocks away from here."

We walk to the Sharewheels car and Frankie keys in a code on the panel. The device beeps, and the number *five* appears on the screen in brightly lit letters. A little hatch opens and Frankie plucks out the car keys.

"Whose code was that? How do you know they won't trace us?"

Frankie doesn't look at me. "It's a code used by Riff's group. The guy who owned it died two years ago. It's for emergencies only and can't be traced back to me." Frankie ducks into the car parked in bay five. "You coming or what?"

I get into the passenger seat. She starts the car, and we hit the road again.

"I'll take you to Rotterdam and drop you off at home," Frankie says.

The idea of saying goodbye to her stings much more than I'm ready to admit, but I also have no idea whether it's smart to keep her in my life. Will I ever be able to look at her again—at her beautiful eyes, the dimple in her cheek, her full lips—and not feel remnants of betrayal?

"Why didn't you leave when I told you to?" Her soft voice cuts through the hum of the car's electric engine.

"I realized that if I just stood by and did nothing, I'd be no better than the people who cheer for Vallance. Isn't there an old quote for that? Something like: all evil needs to win is for good people to do nothing?" I sigh. "I just... didn't want to stand at the sidelines anymore."

"I thought..." Frankie trails off, then nods. "Can I turn on the radio?"

"Sure."

Crackling sounds bubble up from the small speakers on the dashboard. I press some buttons at random, and a female voice suddenly reverberates through the car.

"Today's attack was an attack on all of us. Vallance defended himself bravely, but by not giving in to the demands of the unhinged criminals trying to undermine our democracy, he gave his life for ours." The woman pauses. "We will now listen to Chairman Hawking speaking to reporters at a press conference."

Vallance is officially dead.

A deep male voice takes over. "Today will go down in the books as a dark day for our country. We will carry the loss of our beloved president with us forever." A pause, a chance. "But today is also a victory. "The perpetrators have been caught. Their plans to turn our nation back into a haven for criminals like themselves have failed. We are certain that this was only a small, radical group, and all members were killed during their cowardly attempt."

Several voices pipe up in the background, intermingling until one rises above the din.

"How were they able to get so close to the president?"

Chairman Hawking clears his throat. "There's still much investigation to be done, but we have reason to believe that President Vallance's makeup artist was in on the assassination. He went to college with one of Vallance's personal guards, who was also involved. Both men paid for this with their lives. You can rest assured that starting today, the screening process for the president's immediate staff will be even more rigorous."

"Speaking of the president," a woman says in a mournful voice, "who will take over for Vallance and help us through this difficult time?"

"This afternoon at exactly five o'clock, a three-day national mourning period will commence. We ask that people stay indoors to grieve this terrible loss."

I realize that a ban on being outside creates the perfect opportunity for the Guard to track us down.

"We are lucky that our president always had a backup plan," the chairman continues. "He had already named his successor, who will be announced this afternoon at five o'clock. We kindly ask everyone to use their time until then to head home and switch on their TVs. At five o'clock, we'll also share more information about this official mourning period."

Frankie turns the radio off. "If we stick to the speed limit, we'll be in Rotterdam in under an hour. I won't be able to travel far after then, before five o'clock comes around." She casts me a hesitant glance. "Do you think I could maybe... hide at your place for the time being?"

I may be a little resentful, but I'm not cruel. "I'm not gonna kick you to the streets."

When we turn down my family's road, it feels like I never left. But it also feels like I'm entering a totally new world at the same time. The street hasn't changed, nor has my house—but *I* have.

Frankie parks the car in the Sharewheels a bit farther down the road. We walk to the front door without speaking. My legs want to run, but the few people I see outside have their head hanging low, so I force myself to slow, as though I'm grieving too.

Once we're in front of the door, I take a deep breath and knock three times in quick succession. That's how Cross knows it's me.

The door swings open, and a few tufts of blond hair poke out from behind it. I can't contain myself anymore. I dash at my little brother, making him stumble back as I pull him into my warm embrace. I faintly register Frankie stepping in and shutting the door behind us.

"Sinny!" Cross hugs me back. "Where *were* you?"

I pull back and give him a puzzled look. "Didn't Dad tell you anything?"

Cross rolls his eyes. "He tells me all kinds of things. *You shouldn't whine, Cross. Don't ask so many questions, Cross. Of course Sin will come back. Your sister can take care of herself just fine.* Yada, yada."

I smile, tears welling up in my eyes. "And where is he now?"

He shrugs. "He went somewhere."

I scan the living room. There's a half-finished bag of chips on the coffee table next to a stack of old comic books.

"Cross? How long has Dad been gone?"

"Dunno. Why do you have hair like a soldier? And who is *that*? You want some chips?"

I don't respond to his questions. Cross only eats chips when he gets really hungry and no one's home. Something's not right here.

Cross plops down onto the couch and grabs the remote. The TV comes to life, and a serious-looking man with gray hair appears on screen. Out of the corner of my eye, I see Frankie freeze.

"Good evening. My name is Jonathan Hawking, and it is with a painful heart that I address you all tonight. Our beloved president was killed this afternoon in a horrific and cowardly manner, by terrorists who seek to destroy our way of life by spreading fear and division." Hawking raises a fist. "But they have underestimated us. They have no idea how strong we are. Our solidarity and loyalty toward each other, and our country, are unwavering. As long as we have each other, nothing can defeat us."

Cheers rise up from an audience offscreen.

"At the request of President Vallance, I will take over his position. The many conversations I had with him will support me in this difficult task. I'm sure we will all come out of this ordeal stronger. The perpetrators have been caught. They will never again threaten your safety. Please watch the video footage captured earlier this evening."

I try to swallow the lump in my throat and turn my head away from the violent images on the TV. "Cross... Did Dad mention where he was going?"

"To work, I think. He said he was going to take a bull by the horns, or something?"

I think my insides just turned upside down.

"Oh, wait!" Cross points excitedly to the screen. "Dad's not at work after all! He's on TV."

FORTY-FIVE

I snatch the remote from Cross and turn up the volume.

On screen, I see my father in a long line of people, his arms cuffed behind his back. His face is blank.

"Riots have broken out in several cities around the country following the attack, by criminals trying to take advantage of our mourning. They are rioters who seek to seize power for themselves, but all of them have underestimated the strength of the Netherlands, the strength of our Guard —and above all, the strength of unity."

The Guard throws them into the armored vans. There's only one place they could be headed.

The Drain.

Beside me, Cross gently rocks back and forth.

I put my hand on his shoulder. "Cross?"

"Not everything you see on TV is real, right?" With teary eyes, he looks up at me. "Superman can't really fly. And nobody really gets all big and green like the Hulk. Not everything we see on TV is real."

I hug him and stroke his back, just like I used to do whenever he got scared of the dark. Frankie turns the volume off and the captions on. We watch in silence as several masked people run after the Guard's vans. It looks like they overpower them, but before the fight ends, the transmission cuts off, faltering for a moment before Hawking comes back into frame.

I look at Frankie helplessly. *What should we do now?*

Determined, she turns off the TV, then the lights. I keep hugging Cross.

"Your father was arrested, your brother doesn't officially exist, and you allegedly didn't survive the Hangar." She goes into the kitchen and pulls the drapes closed. "So there's no reason for anyone to be in here. If there's a light on, it'll be suspicious."

"But what should we *do*?"

"We have to get through the next three days without anyone noticing that we're here."

I leave Cross alone for a few minutes to help Frankie close every curtain in the house. I bring the comic books to Cross's room—the one farthest from the front door—and then fetch him next.

"We're going to camp out in your room for a while, okay? All three of us. Reading comics, eating good food, having slumber parties..."

Cross nods, but I still see the fear in his eyes as I lead him to the bedroom.

"It'll be alright. Everything's going to be okay." I sit down on his bed and pat the space next to me. My little brother sits down, his shoulders hanging.

"I was gone for a while, right? Way too long. But it wasn't my choice."

"Why not?" he asks timidly.

"Those were the rules. Just like how you're not allowed to go outside."

Cross nods. He's lived by those rules for his entire life.

"But in that place where I was, I learned something."

"Building robots?"

"No, something much better."

"Better than robots?"

"Yes!" I grab his hands and stare into his deep blue eyes. I tell him about Q's secret place. About the vegetable garden and the itchy bugs. About the free people. About how everyone is allowed to be themselves. A place without registrations. A place full of hope. I tell him, but maybe I tell myself even more.

As Cross drifts off to sleep, I think of death. Mia. Jonah. Potentially my dad.

Was it all for nothing?

Cross turns onto his back and begins to snore. His face is completely relaxed now.

At least I'm reunited with my brother again. He seems to be doing okay. Maybe the medicine hasn't fully run out yet. We'll figure something out. We always do.

Frankie is sitting against the wall across from me, arms crossed. Her lips are pinched together, and her forehead is creased into a deep frown. She looks like she expects the doorbell to ring at any moment.

I wipe Cross's hair away from his face, then sit next to Frankie.

Her voice trembles. "What if I was wrong?"

"About what?"

"What if I just made everything worse?" Frankie looks at me with her piercing gaze. "I'm scared, Sin. What if it never mattered *why* I did it?" She takes a deep breath and blinks rapidly to fend off tears. "Am I a monster?"

I place my hand on her thigh, meet her gaze, and really take her in. Right now, I *see* her. I see the girl I fell in love with, who always fights for what she believes in.

I see the pain in her eyes, the sadness, the regret...

"You're not a monster," I say, and I mean it. "And things have changed. You saw it on TV. People are rebelling. For the first time in years, they're resisting his regime. Of course it won't all change at once, but I think you set the first cogs going. Now we can only hope they'll keep turning, to set even larger wheels into motion."

Frankie shakes her head and grabs both of my hands. "I'm really sorry, Sin. If I could turn back time, I'd be honest about everything."

"It's okay. We can't redo the past. All we can do is learn from it. Help each other to do better. Help others not to make the same mistakes. Small steps."

Frankie smiles weakly. "Maybe it was naive to think that I could really change anything, that I could kill all my demons in one fell swoop. I just wanted it so badly. I *wanted* there to be a point to everything, to prove him wrong—all the times he said I wasn't strong enough, good enough, smart enough. All the times he said I didn't have it in me." She doesn't hold back her tears anymore—they drip from her chin onto her legs. "I wanted him to be wrong. I don't want to feel so small anymore."

"I don't understand how someone like you could ever believe that you're small. Our whole little tribe in the Hangar looked up to you. Mia, Lynn,

Nora, Q—even the Long-Termers, though they'd never admit it. That jerk *Riff* too." I pause. "What I'm trying to say is that you can't change the world without changing people. The people whose lives you touch, in turn, help others—and so it goes on and on. Kind of like an oil slick that keeps spreading." The next words leave my lips before I've really thought them through. "Please join Cross and me. Let's find Q's hiding place."

Hope sparks in her red-rimmed eyes. "Are you serious?"

I lean forward and press my lips to hers. "Absolutely."

EPILOGUE

I pick dark purple berries from the bush and gently drop them into my bucket. The soft rays of early autumn make it the perfect temperature outdoors.

Some distance away, Cross laughs heartily. He stomps his feet, then quickly lies on his stomach, smudging his cheek with dirt as he stares down in concentration. He's looking for worms to help out the fishermen—he's really found his niche here. Cross has the patience of an angel and an almost eerie gift for tracking down those wriggling creatures.

He hardly goes inside.

Frankie, Cross, and I have been living with this group for about three weeks now. It proved more difficult than we expected to follow clues and figure out where the rebels were hiding. We're located on the eastern side of the Netherlands, just far enough from Germany to keep our distance from border control officers. The people here remembered Q, and as a friend of hers, they accepted us into their group.

We have our own place. It's a little house partly underground, hidden under a fallen tree. It's invisible to the drones that occasionally pass overhead. The three of us share a small living room—where Cross sleeps—and two bedrooms for Frankie and me. It's more than I could ever dream of, and after my time in the Hangar, it feels like pure luxury.

During the day, we help on the fields, and in the evening, we often sit around the campfire to discuss preparations for the coming winter.

From time to time, I hear whispers about the world outside our commune.

Rumors say that President Hawking is having great difficulty running the same tight ship that Vallance did. More and more, revolts take place, and people are talking about organizing a new election.

Within the confines of our smaller world, though, no one seems to care. With over forty people, young and old, we work toward the same goal. For the first time, I feel like I'm finally home.

That doesn't mean everything's easy. We're still in hiding. We're still afraid sometimes. I spend a lot of nights without sleep, replaying the TV screen in my head, watching the Guard take Dad away. Cross convinced himself that the masked rioters rescued him. I'm not so sure. Sometimes I have nightmares about him working himself to death in the Drain. On nights like those, I curl up against Frankie in her bed. I don't have to explain anything. She does the same with me just as often.

My bucket is full of berries, and I straighten up, stretching my neck. Two warm hands slip around my shoulders and gently massage them.

Frankie presses a kiss to my cheek. "Those look delicious." She reaches for the bucket, and I swat her hand playfully.

"Those are for dinner."

She frowns, and I lean in to kiss her.

"Are you feeling any better?" I ask, remembering last night. She was having trouble sleeping.

"Oh, I'm fine now. Just glad we're here." She sighs and rests her head on my shoulder. "Every day I get a little better. Small steps."

"Sin! Frankie!" Cross comes running after us. His face is bright red, and his clothes are stained, but he's still beaming. He holds out something small and black—it's our camp's community flip phone, used only for emergencies. "Someone wants to talk to you."

I frown and take the phone. "Hello?"

"Sin! It really *is* you!" Q's voice blares through the speaker. I have to hold it a bit away from my ear to keep from going deaf. "Hey Nora, I've got Sin on the phone! Oh my God. Are you okay?"

I smile. "Yeah, all good. I'm with Frankie and my brother. How about you?"

Q laughs. "We're great. Just crossed the border."

"How are you even calling us?"

"Ramon has a non-traceable phone."

"Okay, but how did you get this number?"

"I made sure to remember my old camp's number all this time, in case they brought it when they fled. Thought I'd check in with them, and what do you know? Now I'm talking to you! You found them! Although, it's too bad you're not coming to Belgium."

So that's why I used to hear Q mumbling numbers in the Hangar...

For the next few minutes, she tells me about their journey, about how different things are in Belgium, about European Union talks to support the Dutch people. We promise to stay in touch and to see each other again as soon as we can.

With tears in my eyes, I hang up the phone.

"We did it," Frankie says. From the look in her eyes, I can tell she's truly proud. "We really did change things. We'll get there eventually."

I wrap my arms around her and bring her close. Her body is warm against mine.

When we pull away, I cup her cheek with my hand and look her deep in the eyes.

"Yes." I smile. "Small steps."

Get Ʒost. in bonus content for *Wallbound*

Explore deleted scenes, author interviews, artwork, and more

LOSTISLANDPRESS.COM

ABOUT THE AUTHOR

RUBY COENE has her own practice in Utrecht, where she works as a child and adolescent therapist. In addition to her work, she loves reading, traveling, and writing fiction. Her debut *Sahana* is a gritty YA dystopian novel about finding hope in the darkest of times, and her sophomore YA novel *Wallbound* was favorably received by bloggers and librarians in the Netherlands under its original Dutch title *Muurvast*. She also writes contemporary fantasy books for children.

ALSO FROM LOST ISLAND

LONE PLAYER
JULIA ROSEMARY TURK

To manage overpopulation, citizens are marked with playing card tattoos—and an annual draw from a deck determines who the Chaser Corps exterminates.

THE MEMORY JUMPER
AMANDA MICHELLE BROWN

Adelaide, an illegal Memory Jumper, lives in an underground safe house with a narcissistic mother who secretly exploits her mind-altering powers for money.

MY BROTHER'S SPARE
SHIRA BEHORE

Valeria's secret investigation to find her mother's murderer pulls her into an alliance with Alias Black, the most infamous hitman in the kingdom.

ABOUT THE PUBLISHER

LOST ISLAND PRESS is an independent publisher of dystopian, sci-fi, and fantasy books. Unlike mainstream presses, we don't publish everything for everyone. We publish for *you*. Our catalog offers grounded, character-driven stories that linger long after the last page. The kind you get lost in, that keep you up at night. And because our books have the same vibe, if you enjoy one, you'll enjoy them all.

LOSTISLANDPRESS.COM
Join our newsletter to claim a free ebook